A Story That's Been Told A Thousand Times

By Marie Joseph-Charles

For my mother, Jill Marie, who gave me independence

For my Grandpa, Justin Joseph, who gave me love

For my uncle James Charles, who gave me wisdom

ISBN/SKU:9780578555317

ISBN Complete:978-0-578-55531-7

Marie Joseph-Charles 2

Epilogue: By Suzanne

It's a story that has been told a thousand times in life and fiction. There were Antony and Cleopatra, Catherine the Great and Grigory Potemkin, Henry VIII and… well, most of his wives. They were some of the most amazing couples in history and they all started while one of them was already married. Authors and movie makers have romanticized the idea of star-crossed lovers who find each other. Society, while enthralled with these stories, still frowns on the practice in general.

I never really saw myself as the type of woman to cheat on her husband. In truth, I hadn't realized I had a reason to. We were happy for the most part. At least, I thought we were. I feel comfortable using the word 'complacent." Keith and I had virtually nothing in common and yet some how managed to weave a tangled but functional marriage knot for quite some time. A little romantic gesture such as coming home to a clean house every once in a while would have been nice. His idea of romantic was holding in a fart until he was safely in the next room. While I appreciated the gesture, something a little deeper would have been a welcome change.

When we first met, I had nothing that could be even remotely construed as a attraction to him. He was short and stocky, but otherwise ordinary and maybe even a little homely. As our years together progressed, his ordinary physique fell into disrepair. Twenty years of smoking had left him with a horrible hacking cough that was so regular, he didn't even notice. His profession required him to sit at a desk in a windowless office all day so his belly steadily grew more protuberant as years passed until he reached the point that doctors refer to as 'obese'. He would let his hair grow into an unmanaged mop that melded into a rarely-trimmed beard. Due to this and his constant wear of the same clothes, he frequently resembled a well-off hobo. He didn't make much money for as much time as he spent working, but that's not why I married him. We were blissfully middle-class.

We met when we were in our early twenties. We had an overlapping group of friends and frequently ran into each other.

Marie Joseph-Charles 3

Somehow, spending so much time together nurtured something that resembled a romantic relationship.

One of our mutual friends (the one who introduced us) was Frank. She was my soul sister. We had met in college and attended vet school at the same time. She moved away to further her career and to start a family, but we remained close. She had everything- blonde hair, blue eyes, brains, and boobs. She was fun and outgoing and loved life. I am her polar opposite in every way conceivable.

I wasn't the biggest fan of her (now ex) husband. He treated her well and made her happy and that should have been all that mattered. But every time I was near him, something just felt… off. It turns out I was right, but we'll get into that later. They had a house in the middle of suburbia the next state over where they raised Amber, Christina, and Chad (Brian had to have a son). To outsiders, theirs was the fairytale life that every little girl hopes for.

Then there was Ian. Ian was my husband's best friend. He was best man at our wedding and chosen god father to any children we may have had. He was tall, dark, and average. He was lean and lanky with a permanent tan from his outdoor hobbies and summer work as a landscaper. To be truthful, I had more in common with Ian than I did my husband from the beginning. While Keith enjoyed watching TV in his bathrobe and his idea of getting outdoors was working on his collector's car in the garage, Ian and I enjoyed hiking and camping. We would text each other pictures if we found a particularly beautiful view or swap tips for off-the-path hideaways. He had a brilliant intellect and I loved when he would come visit so I could have someone to discuss books with (my husband was most definitely NOT well-read).

I'm getting ahead of myself. We should probably start this whole thing from the beginning.

My Side: By Ian

Before you judge me let me explain something. Suzanne and Keith were already dating when I met her. I am not the kind of guy that goes and ruins his best friend's relationship just because he's attracted to his girl. I mean, okay, yes I thought (and still think) she's beautiful and smart and funny and successful… No, I didn't think he deserved her but neither did I. I was just a schlub in a tiny apartment and still in college. What did I have to offer her?

I had seen her pictures a lot but when I first met her, she was really shy. Keith explained later that she was coming out of an abusive relationship where the guy basically told her she was useless and worthless and wouldn't let her interact with other people. I'd liked to have had a conversation of my own with that guy but last I'd heard he'd been arrested for abusing another woman.

Anyways, the night I first met her, we were at a bonfire at Frank's house. The whole night she sat all quiet with a bottle of water in her hand. She would only speak if spoken to. I noticed her laugh quietly to herself instead of just letting it out and being a part of the fun if someone said something funny. Needless to say, I thought she was pretty but weird. I didn't know her history at the time. It took a couple of times meeting her before I realized there was a really deep person in there.

Keith moved into her house pretty quickly after they started dating. I guess she needed help with bills. She was commuting pretty far for school and since she was a full time student with two part time jobs, she appreciated a little help.

He's lucky he was my best friend because I seriously hate helping people move and moving in December made it worse. The day he moved in, I was helping him carry his dresser and complaining about school. "I don't know why I have to take this stupid biology class. What does it have to do with architecture? I'm supposed to make a detailed diagram describing the Crab's Cycle for class on Monday." I didn't even notice her sneak up behind me with drinks in her hands as I complained.

Marie Joseph-Charles 5

"You mean the Krebs Cycle." She scared the shit out of me and I think she knew it as she smiled and handed me a cold can of Mountain Dew. "It describes the reactions that cells use to generate energy during aerobic respiration. Carbon dioxide and water are waste products produced in the mitochondria and adenosine *di*phosphate is converted to adenosine *tri*phosphate."

I kind of stared at her with my mouth open for a second. "How on earth do you understand that?"

"Unlike you, I *am* a biology major."

I suddenly remembered that she planned to be a veterinarian and realized how stupid my question was. "So do you want to do my homework for me?"

She smiled and got a look on her face that was, like, mocking deep thought. "Professor Stueben?"

"Yeah! You had him?"

"I did my first two years locally to save money. Yeah, I had him. He gave me an A- on that assignment. He said it was well researched but lacked creativity in my explanation. What does that even mean? Sorry, Love. You're on your own." She turned and headed back to the kitchen.

I had to laugh. They had been dating for something like a year at that point and that was the most interaction I'd had with her.

Marie Joseph-Charles 6

How I met my Sister: By Suzanne

So, we were all pretty broke college kids in the beginning. Frank and Brian hadn't met yet. She was the smart one of the two of us. She lived in a cramped, overcrowded apartment near the main campus when we first met. It was expensive, but she didn't have the ninety-minute commute in rush hour traffic in the morning and up to two hour commute to get back (there were always accidents in the afternoon.) She grew up in the next school district over from me and at one point we found a picture of a middle school softball game where we had played against each other. Our moms even worked in the same office building when we were small children (though my mom was a temporary cleaning lady and hers was some type of project manager). We joked that it was fate trying to introduce us. We didn't actually meet and become friends until our third year of pre-vet.

She had decided to complete all four years at main campus so we didn't meet until I transferred from the community campus. Our charming school mandated that at least two years of any four-year program had to be completed at main campus even though the same classes were offered at the much cheaper community campus. My program advisor said it was so that I would have access to the department heads, better library, etc. Whatever.

I walked in to the first day of organic chemistry and the only open seat was next to this strawberry blonde Barbie doll. Great. All I needed in my life was a pre-med airhead who was out to save the world as my lab partner for a whole semester. I sat down and politely smiled as I set down my bag and placed my books on the lab bench.

She turned to me. "Hi! I'm Frank!" She had the biggest smile with the whitest teeth I had ever seen. It made her unnaturally blue eyes scrunch and duck behind the longest natural eye lashes I had ever seen.

"Suzanne." I shook her outstretched hand.

"I'm pre-vet. You?"

"The same."

Marie Joseph-Charles 7

"Oh! Great! Everyone I've met has been either nursing or pre-med. I've met a couple other pre-vet, but they were the whole," her voice suddenly switched to the total valley-girl I had stereotyped her as "'I'm going to be a vet because I like animals' type." She rolled her eyes. "Total waste of time and money for them. They have no idea what they are getting into." She looked me up and down. "You look a bit more realistic. You have this *vibe*."

"Uh. Thanks. I think." She was sarcastic and snarky. That was the moment I knew I had found a kindred spirit.

Just as she opened her mouth to say something else, this sad, skinny, disheveled looking man shuffled in with a coffee and an arm full of folders and papers. He set everything but the coffee on a table in front of the class and cleared his throat. He stood at the front of the class and took a deep breath. "Good morning. I'm Professor Cane." He took a long, deep gulp of coffee. I could see the steam from where I was sitting. He had to have an esophagus made of steel to not get third degree burns from that. He set the mug down. "Look. I don't care if you come to lecture. It's your choice. Some students do fine studying on their own and I'm good with that. But if you don't come to class, don't waste my office hours trying to get one-on-one lecture time. I'll tell you you're S.O.L. For those of you who come to class and still struggle, my office hours are on your syllabus in your class portal online. You are welcome to come talk to me. You have three minor exams totaling thirty-three percent of your over all lecture grade and one final exam totaling sixty-seven percent of your final lecture grade. These are the only days that are mandatory. At five after I lock the classroom door. If you aren't in this room, you get a zero on the exam. No exceptions. And don't think you can come strolling in any time you please on non-exam days. I'm good with faces and I remember students who disturb the learning experience for the rest of the class."

As I'm listening to him talk, I can feel my anxiety building. I wasn't good at chemistry in high school and the thought that one exam was worth two-thirds of our grade and I had punctuality problems… I worked a second-shift data entry job and third shift

at an emergency veterinary clinic. I tried to discretely check my
pill case to make sure I had taken my morning meds.

I think Frank noticed my sudden change comfort. She
nudged me with her elbow. "Don't worry. We got this." She was
still facing the front of the class but smiling just as bright as ever.

Just then I heard "All lab days are mandatory. There are
absolutely *no* lab make-ups and, again, the door locks at five
after."

I looked down at the syllabus I had printed that morning. I
had an inherent distrust of technology. This was back in 2005 and
I was 21 years old. I was young enough to appreciate my laptop
but old enough to be used to surviving without it. The syllabus
clearly stated that lab ended at 5p.m. on Thursdays. Okay. I had
to be at the processing center at 7p.m. No work conflict. I took a
deep breath. Lecture days were my only worry. Class started at
nine. My shift at the emergency clinic was scheduled to end at
eight but I rarely left on time. In good traffic it was a twenty
minute drive to the school. It was an average five to seven minutes
to find parking on campus and another five minutes to sprint to
class if I found a spot in the green lot or eleven minutes if I had to
park in the blue lot.

I had run all of these calculations before when I was
scheduling my classes but my anxiety was sending me into panic
mode. I could not be late. I would actually *physically* be locked
out of class if I was late. Well, on exam days I would be locked
out. But if I didn't show that I could be punctual, maybe he
wouldn't let me schedule office hours help… By this point I had
tuned out the instructor and was lost in my own little world of
panic.

I was right to panic. The next morning I left the clinic at
8:17a.m.. It took me twenty-six minutes to get to campus. As luck
would have it, it only took me four minutes to find a spot but it was
in the blue lot. Two minutes to grab my stuff and start to run but I
had to double back when I realized I grabbed my work bag instead
of my school bag. That wasted another four minutes and it took
me eleven minutes to sprint across the green. I dipped through the

door just as Cane was closing it. His watch is one minute faster than mine. Good to know.

I was still in my scrubs from work. I was out of breath and covered in German Shepard hair. I could smell the dried urine in my pants and I didn't dare let anyone know I had found a cat turd in my pocket when I put my keys in it.

After twelve years in grade school, it amazes me how assigned seating is engrained into a scholarly habit. I instinctively took my seat next to Frank before I looked around and realized that of the nearly fifty students that had been there the day before, there were only 8 of us in attendance. She looked at me wide eyed. I opened my mouth to apologize for my pungent presence and offer to move but before I could say anything she asked "Where do you work and how do I get a job there?"

All I could do was laugh.

It had turned out that we had a lot of the same classes and our strengths and weaknesses were inverse of each other. She was good at chemistry and I was good at physics. We used our lunch hour to cram-tutor each other and I ended up getting her a job at the veterinary clinic with me. She only worked on the weekends so she could focus on school but we used down time at work to help each other.

We were a great team and even better friends. Opposites really do attract. She stayed at my house on the weekends for work (even though her family was only fifteen minutes away) and I had a place at Sunday dinner at her family's house. One Sunday in January of 2006, there was an extra guest. He was Frank's next door neighbor growing up and he had just moved back into town. I shook his hand. "Hi. I'm Keith."

Just Three Kids: By Ian

I grew up across the street from Keith and Frank. Frank and I got along really well. It's impossible to not get along with her. She has that kind of personality that sucks you in in a good way. I really didn't like Keith at first. He was kind of a trouble maker. He did things like throw fire crackers and M80s at random things (not usually *his* things) just to see what would happen. He and Frank went to the public schools while I went to the private schools. I'm not saying that made me better but I did have a little more structure and self control. The big thing was, I really wasn't around him all that much to get to know him until we were eleven.

Frank was out front serenading the neighborhood with her flute. It kind of sounded like screams of terror mixed with dying baby birds. Her parents had encouraged her to join the school band but realized that it was going to take practice and a lot of it before they could stand the sound so they made her practice outside. The rest of the neighborhood wasn't too happy about that. She had a lot of talents but this wasn't one that came naturally to her.

I looked out my window and saw a sad little blonde girl with a flute and a book trying to sort things out. I felt bad for her. She was my friend. Damn it. I grabbed my violin and went outside and across the street.

Her eyes lit up. "You play the violin?"

"Since I was five. Don't you dare tell anyone." I sat down next to her.

I looked at her sheet music. It was the standard Mary Had a Little Lamb starter stuff. Piece of cake. I helped her read it and we practiced the notes and chords together for about an hour.

"Hey! Me too!" I looked up and saw Keith coming out of his house with a guitar.

"Can you play that thing?" I was a little skeptical.

"My dad is in a band. He taught me and my step brother. We play together when I go over there every other week." He sat on the other side of Frank.

Marie Joseph-Charles 11

"I would expect someone like you to play the drums." I wasn't lying. From what I knew of him, pounding on something seemed right up his alley.

"Where's the challenge in hitting stuff with sticks? What are we playing?" He pulled over the sheet music. "Easy!"

We sat out there for hours. A flute, a violin, and a guitar were playing nursery songs in unison. It sounded awful but it was fun. Frank started to feel more confident and could understand what she was reading.

After that, we started to spend a lot more time together. We did our homework together in each other's kitchens. Well, Frank and I did homework. Keith made sculptures out of school supplies or played on his handheld videogames more often than not. I loved when we worked at Keith's house though. His mom let us have pop and packaged cupcakes for snacks. Those things were treats in my house but his mom couldn't cook and, truthfully, didn't really care what he ate or did. He was kind of a bad influence on me.

We really became close as we grew up. They came to all of my basketball games, some of my mathletes competitions, and pretty much every major event in my life. I went to pretty much all of Frank's band concerts, cheerleading competitions, academic decathlon meets, softball games…she was into a lot of stuff. Keith was there for both of us. Extracurriculars weren't really 'his thing.' He was the best cheerleader we could ask for though; he almost always brought a whistle or airhorn or some other obnoxious noisemaker to make sure we could hear him over the crowd. Not really appropriate at academic decathlon or mathletes but we appreciated his enthusiasm.

In the eighth grade, when Frank really, um, 'developed,' Keith got a fleeting crush on her. She told him that they could never date. As much as she loved him, he wasn't going anywhere in life and that wasn't what she wanted. Ouch. He took it well enough and moved on to the next piece of ass he could chase. When we were in high school, my friends at my school would see them come watch my basketball games and they always asked why I wasn't dating the 'hot blonde.' The fact was I couldn't. I didn't see her like that. She was a sister to me. We were our own little fucked up family and I loved it. I will admit, we got into her mom's liquor cabinet once when we were like, fifteen, and drunkenly made a marriage pact but no one knew about it but us. For a long time, I didn't even know she remembered doing it.

Frank did waste like, three years in high school and just after with this total tool named Wayne. Keith and I hated him. She knew we hated him. He was this horrible, whiny, little mama's boy. He was short, fat, and had buggy eyes. When he cheated on her – still don't know how he found a second high school girl to sleep with him – Keith and I cornered him in the bathroom and threatened to maim him if he didn't come clean.

I was there to watch Frank give a speech for a debate competition and Keith and I saw him get up to pee. At seventeen and sixteen years old, I was six feet and one inch tall and had a bit of muscle but Keith was built like a fucking rock. Wayne saw us when we followed him in. He turned to face us. I backed him into a wall and stood over him. He looked passed me. Keith was standing in the doorway with his arms crossed. He was wide enough to almost fill the door frame. There was no way Wayne was getting passed him. We calmly explained to Wayne that if he didn't tell Frank what he had done, he would find himself duct-taped to the flagpole out front with an M80 zip-tied to his penis. He cried and I'm pretty sure he wet himself a little.

We left the bathroom pretty happy with ourselves. Apparently, that was the wrong thing to do. After Frank's speech, he told her what he had done. She actually *forgave* him for his 'moment of weakness.' Are you kidding me? Then she told us how disappointed she was with how we handled it. My heart sank when she used that word. I felt like I was being scolded by my mother. It was awful. After she was done laying into us, she smiled, kissed us each on the cheek, and thanked us for having her back. They wound up breaking up when he cheated on her for like the fourth or fifth time when we were in college.

She was always screening and scrutinizing our girlfriends but I guess she handled things with a bit more subtlety. Keith wasn't really serious about a lot of things and girlfriends were on that list. I think the longest relationship he was in (before he met Crazy Chick) was when we were juniors and it lasted like two

Marie Joseph-Charles 13

months. His criteria were simple enough. They had to be female, an easy lay, and the distance between her waist and her belly button couldn't be wider than his hand because he 'didn't do fatties.' Every girl I brought home would leave shortly after meeting Frank. Some said they felt like they couldn't compete with her. What the Hell? I wasn't dating her and had no plans to. I did find one girlfriend in college with staying power but it just wasn't meant to be.

     Life is weird. When you're in high school, you think it's your whole world. But then, BAM! It's over and you're a fish out of water trying to breathe and flounder through life. After we graduated, we all had to find our own streams. Keith had fallen head over heals for this seriously crazy chick our senior year. They were only dating for like a month. She was moving across the country be an actress or some other nonsense and he went with her. Frank moved into the city to be closer to her school. I stayed home and worked for a year before I moved north for college. I wasn't there for long when I had to come home when my mom was diagnosed with breast cancer and she needed me.

We called each other whenever something major happened and e-mailed constantly. Social media eventually became big and we tracked each other that way too. Keith and Crazy Chick broke up when she started sleeping with every Tom and Dick who claimed they could get her a part in a commercial. He stayed out there though because he had enrolled in some kind of accounting program. He originally did it so he could get the income from student loans to support himself and Crazy Chick but he ended up liking it. Could have knocked me over with a feather when he announced that one. Frank was still Frank. Can't say I was sad when she and Wayne split.

One day, I was checking social media and I saw a picture of Frank and a really pretty brunette. They were downtown and smiling. I had been so busy with school and family it had been a while since I had seen a Frank smile.

I text messaged her. *"Who's the girl in the picture of you in front of the fountain?"*

She messaged me right back. *"That's Suzanne. She's my new friend at school. She's awesome."*

How Keith and I came to be: By Suzanne

     My high school sweetheart was pure poison. I know that now. Back then, he was my one true love. Young and dumb. There wasn't a lot I wouldn't do for him. Forgot to do his homework and needed to copy mine? Okay. Needed me to rework my schedule to drive him to and from work? No problem. A little money for cigarettes or weed? Whatever you need, Honey. You're right, I need to lose some weight; have my last waffle. If I didn't do what was asked of me, he would tell me how selfish and lazy I was. He would tell me that I clearly didn't love him if I wasn't willing to do little things to help him. How could we have a life together and make big decisions when I let little things get between us? I bought it. I believed it all. I came to hate myself. I became miserable with him as the years went on. But, I couldn't leave him. Where else was I going to meet a guy who wanted to be with someone as ugly and useless as me?

     When I was nineteen, I inherited my grandparents' house when my grandma passed away from cancer. It was small and pretty far from the city, but it was mostly paid off (I had to do a bit of financing) and it was a roof over our heads. He moved in when I did so we could start our life together. In my second year of college, I was working two jobs to support us while he continued to jump from one pathetic job to another. At the last one, he made friends with Jimmy. Jimmy introduced him to cocaine and that's what finally did it. Despite some serious threats, I kicked him out but the emotional and mental damage was done.

     It was a little less than a year later when I met Keith at Frank's family's house. He was nice enough but I found him dull and unalluring. He was explaining how he had completed some associate's accounting degree and moved home to find work. Accounting. How exciting. I left dinner that evening with no intention of giving this mundane little man a second thought. I'm wrong a lot.

     He was at Sunday dinner fairly consistently. Apparently, his mom couldn't cook and he had come over on a regular basis for a real meal since he and Frank were little. Frank and I would eek out time to have drinks at a bar with a group of her friends or rent a movie. He would always be there. The more time I spent with him, the more I realized he wasn't so bad. The boring good-guy act he put on at family dinner was just that. He had a dark sense of humor that I appreciated. He always had stories to tell that were actually entertaining.

One night we were all at Frank's favorite bar near campus. It was crowded enough that it had to be some kind of fire code violation. The sardine-can feel combined with the over-loud music kicked my anxiety into overdrive. I excused myself (not that I thought anyone heard me) and slipped out the back door and onto the patio area facing the alley. It was a clear, warm June night in 2006. There were a few smokers out there and a couple making out against the wall, but it was otherwise secluded and I began to do my breathing exercises like the pathetic nerd I am.

Keith came out behind me and lit a cigarette. "You okay?"

"Yeah." I turned to face him and leaned against a railing. "Just needed some air."

"Your anxiety getting to you?" He took a long draw off his coffin nail.

"How did you know I have anxiety problems? I've never brought them up and Frank wouldn't tell."

He blew a plume of blue smoke and stepped sideways. "You don't do well in groups of people. Like now. You try to hide it but you always grip something really tight when you start to get stressed. You always smell like lavender and that's an anti-stress aromatherapy thing. You're a perfectionist and you worry a lot and you don't sleep. Do I need to continue?"

"No." I suddenly felt horribly self conscience and turned away from him.

"Hey. It's okay. It's one of the reasons I like you."

I turned back to him and forced myself to smile a little.

He continued. "I was actually hoping to get you alone a little tonight to ask if maybe I could take you to dinner sometime. Just the two of us."

Okay. I was definitely not expecting that. "Um. Sure."

"You don't have to say yes. I don't want a pity date or anything."

Marie Joseph-Charles 17

"No. I didn't mean it like that. You just kind of caught me off guard."

"I'm sorry. I have a habit of jumping at an opportunity and I didn't know if I was going to get you alone again any time soon. I've been wanting to ask you out for a while now."

I think the feeling I had was flattery. I'd never felt it before so I'm not entirely sure.

He smiled at me. "You are usually off of work on Wednesdays, right?"

"Yeah."

"Cool. Pick you up at eight on Wednesday?"

"Okay." I was still a little in shock. What just happened?

"Awesome! I gotta say I'm a little relieved. I didn't know how I was going to handle it if you had said 'no.'"

He held out his elbow. I suddenly realized that I was so focused on what was happening, that my anxiety had subsided. I took his arm and he escorted me back inside.

Wednesday came and he picked me up at my house. I was terrified. I hadn't exactly dated a lot. I had only dated two guys before Wes. I was with him for five years and I hadn't dated anyone since. I was going to totally mess this up and Frank was going to be mad. She was so excited when he told her we were going on a date. She immediately called me and gave me a few key tidbits about his love life over the years, including his belly button to waist ratio rule (which I most definitely did not fit). She ended by stating that I was the first 'decent' girl he's ever asked out and she was excited for both of us. Great. No pressure.

We had dinner at the local Mexican restaurant. I had a margarita to help me lighten up a little. I'm not supposed to mix alcohol with my meds but, what the Hell. He told me about the car he was building in his dad's garage and the new job he had started as an entry-level accountant. He asked me about working at the vet clinic and school. He asked what I want to do when I graduate and my favorite color. I didn't like to talk about myself but I was pretty sure the point of a date was to get to know each other.

After dinner, we went bowling. I was horrible at it. I understood the physics but that didn't mean I was proficient at applying it. I had the strength to back my ball (lifting hundred-pound dogs for a living will do that) but grossly lacked coordination. He, on the other hand, couldn't seem to bowl less than one-sixty. Of course.

At the end of the evening, he walked me to my door. Great. Nothing like the awkwardness of a goodnight kiss. We turned to face each other. We did the customary "I had fun tonight." "Yeah, me too." And…he hugged me. Wait. What? A hug?

"Good night." He looked me in the eyes.

He had to look up a little because I'm taller, but he looked at me deeper than anyone had ever looked at me before. I saw something I couldn't identify in those piercing blue eyes. He pulled me in for one more hug before ducking off my front porch and leaving me standing there completely confused. I knew it had been a while since I had been on a date but what in the Hell just happened?

I went into my house and lay awake all night analyzing the whole evening. Did it really go so bad he didn't want to kiss me? I know I'm awkward but good God. I'm going to be alone forever.

The next morning I was exhausted from staying up all night and stressing over my first- and probably last- date in quite some time. I was groggy and sluggish as I stumbled into my classroom a little early. I sat next to Frank and she was all smiles, as usual. "Spill it!"

I recapped the entire evening for her including the awkward double-hug thing that had happened and how I was sure I blew it.

"He just hugged you? Twice? That's so wonderful!"

I was too tired for mind games. "What the Hell are you talking about?"

"You have to understand Keith. He has *never* dated a girl he couldn't sleep with on the first date. He doesn't know *how* to act around a woman he actually has feelings for 'cause he's never *actually* had them. If he just hugged you it's because he REALLY likes you! This. Is. Adorable."

Marie Joseph-Charles 19

I let that sink in a little as class started. I heard my phone vibrate in my bag. I tried to stealthily remove it and I flipped open the screen. It was a text message from Keith.

"Did you really have fun last night?"

I thought for a second. Yeah. I actually did other than the whole staying up late worrying about things. *"Yes. Did you?"*

"Yes. And good. I was up all night worrying that I had bored you or scared you off."

I giggled a little to myself. *"Not at all."*

"Good. Can I take you out again?"

I suddenly felt like a giddy high school girl. *"Yes."*

"Cool. I'll come up with something and message you later."

"Okay." I closed my phone and put it back in my bag.

Frank leaned over. "Told you." She nudged me with her elbow.

I was smiling like an idiot and I could tell. I didn't care. It had been a long time since I felt like that.

We text messaged back and forth for the next two days. With my work/school schedule and him working his new job, it was sporadic but we replied when we could.

On Saturday morning, Frank and I left third shift from the vet clinic and he was waiting in the parking lot, leaning against his car.

He stood up straight when he saw me and opened the passenger door. "Can I take you to breakfast?"

Was I blushing? I was pretty sure I was blushing. Guys only did things like that in movies. "Sure." There was that idiot-smile creeping on my face.

"This is the cutest thing EVER!" Frank was squealing.

He looked at her and smiled. "Shut up."

That was pretty much it. I was hooked. Was he perfect? No. Was he what I had envisioned for myself? Not even a little. But he was sweet and kind. He would mow my lawn or feed my cat when I had to work late. He seemed to actually enjoy my company when we were together. I liked this attention. I liked the way he made me feel like I had some kind of value. I wasn't used to that and it felt good. It wasn't long before we were officially considered a 'couple.'

One August night that same year, Frank's mom decided she needed a bon fire. Frank's family and some of her friends from the neighborhood were there. I worked my data entry job that night but not the clinic, so I arrived late. There were a lot of people – especially people I didn't know -- and I was uncomfortable. Most of them were drunk and trying to talk to me like they knew me. I'm not good in situations like that. Keith sat next to me and held my hand while I firmly gripped my drink and tried not to freak out.

He was talking to some guy named Mark when he suddenly lit up and pulled himself to his feet. "Holy shit! He *is* alive!"

He walked passed Mark towards the gate. He threw his arms around a tall and not-unattractive man and held him tight for a few seconds. He escorted him over to the fire. "Sit!" He grabbed an empty lawn chair and pulled it up for him. "This is my girlfriend, Suzanne. Suzanne, this is Ian."

I stood and shook his hand. He had huge, rough hands. I started scanning my memory for mention of this guy. Ian. Grew up across the street. 'Private school prince.' Landscaper. Wants to be an architect. Mom has cancer.

He smiled at me. "I recognize you from Frank's pictures."

I suddenly felt ugly. "I've heard a lot about you."

We sat down. The rest of the evening they played catch-up while I sat silently and absorbed the conversation. Ian was a funny guy. And naturally smart. I liked him from the get-go.

Nature vs Behavior: by Suzanne

Keith decided to take me to the zoo one day in July of 2006. It's a bit of a cliché, but I didn't mention it. It's funny how when people find out you work with animals, they assume your favorite places to go are zoos and aquariums. Yeah, they're fun… but let's do something *different.*

We were strolling down the steep hill that was lined with bear enclosures. It was sunny but windy. The air was sweet from cooking and ice cream carts peddling their goods. Somehow we got on the subject of high school.

"I'll admit I was a bit of a man-whore." He was staring down at the ground as he said it.

"Polar opposite," I said. "I had one high school sweetheart. He didn't treat me well but I was young and dumb. I couldn't see the forest for the trees, and I was wearing rose colored glasses, too, I guess."

"Um…"

"It means I couldn't see the whole picture. I was focusing on little things and only the things I chose to see as happy to boot. He was so supportive of me going to school and when things were good, I thought we were really happy. I chose to focus on that and not see how badly he was manipulating me until it was almost too late. I almost married him and I can't imaging how horrible life would be if I had."

"If he was so bad, why did you start dating him in the first place?"

"He wasn't like that in the beginning. He changed."

"People may change their behavior, but their nature is always the same."

"That's a very pessimistic view."

"It's a sad world. My ex-girlfriend showed her true colors after we moved to California together. I was kind of in the same boat as you. She had me wrapped around her little finger and she knew it. It was a long time before I realized that she was easy in high school, which is one of the reasons we met. I shouldn't have believed she would change for me."

"I still don't quite follow your thought. Are you the same guy you were in high school? Do I need to worry about you leaving me for someone thinner or prettier?"

We were standing in front of the sun bear enclosure. He leaned against the rock wall and pulled me against him. He had his hands on my hips and looked me in the eye. "Sleeping around was a behavior, not my nature. You have nothing to worry about. As far as I'm concerned, there is no one prettier than you." He kissed my forehead.

I kind of felt like he had just played a major cop-out card. I decided to let it drop. I felt like he was wrong. People most definitely do change, whether he chose to believe it or not. Besides, at this point, we hadn't been dating long enough for me to have developed anything that I would consider concrete feelings about him so if he did dump me, I wouldn't have been overly heart broken.

A little Dinner: By Ian

When I had to move back home, I kind of felt like my dreams were taking a back seat. My poor mom felt like it was her fault I wasn't going to graduate from the school I wanted to. I was okay with that. I wasn't okay with the fact that my sister could have just as easily made less of a sacrifice to help. She only lived like ten miles from Mom but always had an excuse why she couldn't help bring her to and from doctor's appointments or help manage the house. Dad left ages ago and since my sister was the definition of 'selfish', everything fell on me. My mother was a strong woman. Even when my dad was around she pretty much raised us on her own. I saw no reason why I shouldn't step up and return the care she had given me. The problem was, I was not prepared for how fucking painful it was to see her go through it. She tried to act like she wasn't scared or worried, but I saw right through her. Her pain caused me pain and I would try to run away just to breathe.

I had to work to help with mom's bills and my college stuff. I had to cut back from a full time to a part time student when I changed schools to devote more to her and helping her run the house. That was okay. I could sneak a few hours here and there to go to Suzanne and Keith's house. I worked landscaping during the day on the weekends but evenings could be free sometimes if I worked hard. Suzanne was pretty much always working or sleeping on the weekends while she was in school but I did get to see her here and there. Most of the time when I went over, I helped Keith in the garage. I held things while he welded or tightened bolts or what-have-you. I really wasn't interested in the car he was building and he really wasn't interested in architecture but we did the smile-and-nod bit and enjoyed just hanging out.

One Saturday in February of 2007, I went over to help fill dents in body panels that I'm pretty sure were obtained by some less-than-legal method. I poked my head at the garage but there wasn't anyone in there. I went to the front door and knocked. I didn't see Keith's daily driver outside but he knew I was coming. The door opened and there was Suzanne. I hadn't been expecting her to be home.

She looked just as surprised. "Keith didn't tell me you were coming over. Come on in."

She backed away from the door and started hoping on one food towards the couch. Her right foot was wrapped up in an Ace bandage. She plopped on the couch and put her foot up on the ottoman. That's when I noticed. She was wearing shorts! She never wore shorts. Wow. Her legs weren't bad. She must have noticed me noticing her legs because she grabbed a blanket off the back of the couch to cover up with.

"What happened to you?" I came in and shut the door.

"Where do I begin? I jacked my shoulder doing a full-body take-down on a pissed off rottweiler that we needed to sedate for radiographs. Because my shoulder was jacked, when I slipped on the top of the stairs at school – with a loaded book bag, I might add – I tried to catch myself with my jacked shoulder, it gave out, and I went down the rest of the stairs with my foot bent the wrong way 'round." She took off the ace bandage like a sock to show me a very swollen and very purple ankle. "Frank called in for me and she's working double to cover."

"Can I get you anything?"

"A bag of frozen peas would be awesome."

I went in the kitchen and opened the freezer. "Are lima beans okay?"

"Sure. They may as well be good for something. Keith's the only one in this house who thinks they're edible."

I laughed. I sat on the ottoman and examined her ankle. It looked like a purple baseball. I pulled the blanket down over it and draped the beans over it.

"Thanks, Love." She smiled.

"Where is Keith, anyway?"

"Out getting dinner."

I took a deep breath. "Why? Something smells really good."

"Well, I thought that since this was pretty much our one shot at having a nice dinner together at the table, I made chicken noodle casserole."

"On a busted leg."

"On a busted leg. He came home and said that didn't sound appetizing at all so he went out to get burgers or something." There was something a little broken-hearted about her when she said it.

My stomach rumbled a little and I realized I hadn't eaten yet that day. "Would you like some company?"

Her face lit up a little. "That would be lovely. It should be about done."

She pulled herself up and started to hop towards the kitchen.

"Sit down. I think I can serve a gimp."

She laughed. "Okay. But at least let me set the table."

She reached passed me to open a cabinet. She smelled like flowers. She pulled out some plates and then got some silverware out of a drawer and hopped back to the table.

I opened the oven. "What's the other thing in here?"

"I made a loaf of bread."

"Like from scratch?"

"Yup. All my grandmother's recipes."

"Well, no offence to your grandmother, but there's no way it's as good as my mama's cookin'."

She laughed. "Fair enough. As long it's edible. I'm studying to be a veterinarian, not a chef."

"Homemade bread and casserole. Why the fuck would he not want to eat this?"

"He wasn't in the mood for it, I guess."

I pulled the casserole out and lifted the lid. It basically looked like chicken pot pie with noodles instead of crust. Good thing I like chicken pot pie. I took the plates and gave us each a big heaping spoonful. I set one plate in front of her and one at the empty place at on the other side of the little table for me.

"There's half a bottle of pinot grigio in the fridge if you're interested," she said as she pulled napkins out of a basket on the side of the table.

"Good deal!" I opened a cabinet and took out two wine glasses and a poured us each a little. I sat down and she held up her glass.

"To a home cooked meal!" She smiled

Marie Joseph-Charles 26

I raised my glass. "To good company."

Dinner was really kind of nice. It was the first time I really got to know her. We went to the same school but never saw each other. Her classes were on the other side of campus. I had just decided to get myself seconds when Keith came home.

"What's going on here?" He asked.

Before she could open her mouth, I stood up. "I'm eating your dinner."

"You ready to fix these body panels?"

I looked at Suzanne out of the corner of my eye. "Can I finish eating first?"

"Sure, man. Come out when you're done." He walked passed us and to the garage. He didn't even acknowledge Suzanne.

I looked over at her and she was looking down at her plate and kind of half-assed poking a pea with her fork. I reached for the bread and grabbed another slice to get her attention. "Can I take some of this home? It's obviously not as good as my mom's 'cause no one can cook like her but I'd like to take her some."

She kind of laughed. "Of course."

We sat and ate a little longer. Her cat was staring at us the whole time and it kind of creeped me out. She tried to pick up my plate when we were done but I took it away from her.

"Where I come from, the cook never cleans." I took the plate back from her.

"That place sounds like paradise." She stood up anyway and hopped over to the sink. She gave me a scrub brush and picked up a towel that was hanging on the stove. "You wash. I'll dry."

"Deal."

When we were finishing up the dishes, Keith opened the garage door. "You coming, man, or what?"

"Yeah. I'll be right there." Keith shut the garage door again. I turned to Suzanne. "Do you need anything before I go out there?"

She smiled. "I had the nice sit-down dinner I was hoping for but with better company. What more could I need?"

You're safe here with me: by Suzanne

It wasn't long after Keith had moved in that I started questioning my decision, and more so, my sanity. He wasn't a stranger but we barely knew each other. With him came extra vehicles, a mountain of laundry, a never-ending supply of dirty dishes, a second person using electricity and water… Every day I came home and found a new reason to panic. Then, just when I thought I had reached my limit, he would do something sweet or surprising and I would completely defuse. For some reason, even though it didn't get better, I couldn't bring myself to kick him out of the house.

On beautiful Tuesday afternoon in March of 2007, my professor sent us all an e-mail that she had laryngitis and would not be in that day. Knowing full and well that I should have taken the free hour to get some studying done, I instead decided to take it as a sign that I should steal some 'me time.' No class, Keith was at work, the library was on the other side of campus… it was an omen!

I stowed my book bag in my car and decided to just have a leisurely stroll in serenity. It was bright and the air was so clean. There were tables set up with recruiters for various clubs and causes. Students were running and laughing. There were some clustered in small study groups. It seemed like everyone was trying to take advantage of such a magnificent early spring day. I was smiling to myself and enjoying the atmosphere when I heard *him.*

"Yo! Suz!"

I should have run. I should have screamed. I should have at least kept walking and pretended I didn't hear him. But, no. I didn't do any of those things. I turned towards the voice.

Wes was running across the lawn towards me. Wes. The man I had stupidly given so much of my young life to. I was fifteen when I had fallen for the tall dark-haired, dark-eyed, misfit who sat at the same lunch table as me. At fifteen, love is forever and since we were both outcasts, it seemed like we were just meant to be. The fact that Daddy hated him was just frosting on the teenage rebellion cake.

It took me more than five years to get the courage to finally end our toxic relationship. Even though that had only been a few years before that perfect day, he looked so different. His once fleshy body was now gangly and thin. His vibrant dark eyes were now sunken. Even his hair looked duller and he had grown something like a beard. The drug use that had caused the final rift between us was taking its toll.

He was out of breath when he reached me. He stunk of cigarettes and uncleanliness. I remember being shocked that he still had healthy looking teeth as he smiled at me.

"What are you doing on a college campus? You barely made it out of high school." The curt tone and the snide remark escaped me before I could stop myself. I had to remember that this was the man who had once thrown me into a wall when he was angry.

He looked me straight in the eye. The smile disappeared. "My friend goes here. I'm supposed to meet him."

"Friend or dealer?" Suzanne! What the hell? Shut up! Shut up! Shut up!

"Both. Aren't we feeling particularly bitchy today."

"We didn't exactly shake hands and agree to stay friends the last time we saw each other."

"No. I came home after a fight and all of my stuff was in the front yard and you had changed the locks."

"If I remember correctly, you swore I would pay for dumping you, and I wasn't stupid enough to give you a chance to change my mind."

"You're right. I did make a promise to you, didn't I? And I bet you still live in that same house." He moved his face closer to mine. "Maybe I should keep that promise."

"It would be the first promise you ever kept." Seriously! Suzanne! What the fuck?

He opened his mouth to make a comeback just as I felt myself being pulled backwards a step.

"Is there a problem here?" Saved by Frank!

He looked at her and straightened up. He looked her up and down. "Well, hello Honey." He shot her a sideways smile.

Marie Joseph-Charles 30

She did her fake valley girl smile at him. "Why don't you do me a favor and buzz off you little prick?"

I stifled a giggle.

He turned back to me. "A promise I will keep." He turned his back to us and walked away.

Frank took my arm and we turned back towards the science building. "You okay?"

I took a deep breath. "Yeah. I think so." In reality, my heart was about to explode. There was enough adrenaline running through me to bring the crew of the RMS Titanic back to life. What had just happened? Why did my mouth keep running?

"What did he mean about keeping a promise?" Frank was clearly very concerned. Her usually strong voice was just a little shaky.

I had told her about Wes and our break up due to his drug abuse a long time ago. I now filled her in on his promise to 'make it so no man would ever want me.'

She stopped cold. "What did he mean by that?"

I looked down at the ground. "Is it that hard to figure out?"

"Had he done it before?" Her voice was elevating with a twinge of panic.

"Not if you ask the state of Ohio." There was so much shame running through me when I said that. I had worked myself into a state of pure denial about what he had done to his niece before I had met him.

She grabbed my shoulders and looked me dead in they eye. "You HAVE to tell Keith!"

I pulled her hands down and held them. "It'll be okay. He'll get high and forget about today."

"Suzanne! If you don't tell Keith, I will!" She had one-eightied from panic to anger.

"Okay. Okay." I let go of her hands.

"Promise!"

"I promise." She hugged me and we walked to botany class together… without my book bag.

That night I sat Keith down at the kitchen table. I told him exactly what had happened when Wes and I had broken up and what had occurred at school that day. He stood up and walked to my side of the table. He pulled me to my feet and held me tight.

"I'd like to see him try. You are safe here with me, even if I have to kill him to make sure of that."

Turns out that Wes's threat wasn't anything to worry about. He was arrested that night. Still. I was glad to have Keith to protect me.

Studying with Frank: By Ian

I had agreed to help Frank prep for impending final exams in April of 2007. Her apartment was pretty close to campus. That's a polite way of saying it was an overpriced hole in the wall. There were four women splitting rent on what had once been a two story house. Frank wasn't particularly friends with any of them. One of the women was this lesbian named Tara. She was madly in love with Frank but either Frank ignored her or was completely oblivious. I'm pretty sure it was the first one. There's no way anyone could be in the same room with them and NOT know.

I knocked on the main door. Tara answered. "What do you want?"

"Just here to see Frank."

"You two got a date or something?"

"You know full and well we aren't dating."

"Yeah. Right." She stood to the side and let me in.

One of her other roommates, a horribly overweight chick named Audrey, was sitting in a chair in the living room with a polo shirt on her lap. She had a needle and thread and was staring at the shirt as if she was willing it to fix itself.

"You've been staring at that button for twenty minutes. Just glue it on." Tara slammed the door behind me.

"I've already requested too many uniforms at work. They won't give me any more. I have to figure this out." Audrey looked seriously upset.

I agonized over whether or not to help. I didn't particularly like Audrey but I didn't NOT like her either. I decided to be the good guy, especially to spite the lesbian that hated me.

I stepped up to her. "Can I help?"

Audrey looked up at me. "Can you sew on a button?"

"Yes."

She looked a little iffy but handed me the shirt, button, and needle with thread. I lined up the button and threw a couple of stitches in it. I tied it off in the back and bit off the remaining thread.

Audrey's eyes got wide. "You are a lifesaver!"

Marie Joseph-Charles 33

Tara kind of huffed. "Jack of all trades."

"Being raised by women has its perks."

Frank was at the landing at the top of the stairs. "It's about time you got here. Come on up!"

I fake-smiled at Tara and nodded to Audrey before going up the stairs.

Frank shut the door behind us. Her room was no more than twelve feet by twelve feet. She had managed to pack in a bed, dresser, desk, mini-fridge, microwave… all the essentials to make it into its own little studio apartment minus a bathroom. That was shared by all of them. There were color coded sticky notes all over the walls and stacks of note cards on top of books.

She flopped down on the bed and stared at the ceiling. "I just *can't* get this math!"

"So you called me?"

"Isn't, like, half your major math?"

"Well, yeah, but that doesn't mean I'm any good at it."

"Please! What else are you going to do tonight?"

"I could have had a hot date."

Frank scoffed. "You haven't had a date since… what was her name? Rachel?

"Roquel. That was a disaster."

"It's not your fault. You didn't know she was still dating that guy."

"Brandon. Yeah, that doesn't matter. Apparently, if you are used as a revenge lay, you are the bad guy. I was forever labeled as a cheater and a girlfriend-thief after that."

"That doesn't mean you shouldn't have gotten back on the dating horse and tried again. Instead, you shot it dead."

"I did not. I dated at Cleveland. Just not very many. I had one girl tell me I am too 'nondescript.' English major."

"Ha! That's funny. I just assumed you didn't date because of what happened with Rachel. Either that or my gaydar is really off."

My mind immediately went to the lesbian downstairs. "Well, thanks for that. Your gaydar is not off. I'm as straight as an arrow. Believe me. I just haven't found a woman who shares interests with me. And is single. And doesn't mind dating someone so nondescript."

"You'll find someone. You're not nondescript. You're adorable."

"Great. I'm a teddy bear."

"More like a puppy."

"What the fuck? So I need a fun-loving woman who's attracted to puppies."

"That just sounds creepy."

"You called me a puppy!"

"I just meant that you're fun and cute and energetic. You'll find someone."

"Can we talk about something other than my lack of love life?"

"I should fix you up with Audrey! She's got a great personality!"

I looked at her. She laughed.

"So about that math homework."

Frank sat up. "Fine. Fine." She grabbed a book off the top of the stack on the dresser.

Four hours. I was there for four hours trying to explain middle grade trigonometry. It was kind of refreshing to see Frank struggle with something. You got to remember that we grew up together. For the most part, she was perfect at everything. I know it seems petty. But, you have to remember that we were like brother and sister so, yeah, it was a little petty.

Someone knocked on the door. "Are you two snogging in there?" It was Tara.

I looked at Frank. "Did she really just use the word 'snogging'?"

Frank laughed. "Open the door, Tara."

The door cracked open. "I just wanted to make sure you were okay."

More like making sure I wasn't snogging your secret crush.

"I'm fine, Tara. I promise. He's just helping me with math stuff."

"Okay, then." Tara shut the door behind her.

"Such a big sister." Frank laughed. Okay. Maybe she was kind of oblivious.

At around eleven o'clock, my stomach started getting pretty loud. "I guess I'd better go to yonder burger joint and get something to eat."

Frank laughed. "Yonder?"

"What? Your roommate said 'snogging.,"

She laughed again. "That's fair."

The Greek God with the Sheltie: By Suzanne

I never liked Brian. For years I thought there was something wrong with me because everyone else seemed to love him and I couldn't figure out why I didn't. There was just something about him that rubbed me the wrong way. Any time he stood too close to me at get-togethers, I had to move away. Part of the problem was that he was always so… immaculate. Hair was done, clothes were perfect, and he smelled amazing. It just wasn't natural. I knew his appearance was everything when he did marketing presentations but everything had to be perfect just to come over for dinner and a movie. That wasn't the only problem I had with him, but it definitely bothered me. If only I had known what I know now when they had first met.

Saturday nights are exhausting when you work at an emergency veterinary clinic. People come home from an evening out and find their animals have eaten God only knows what. Illnesses that owners put off during the week suddenly need to be seen immediately. And, of course, there are the typical overnight emergencies such as hit-by-cars, GDVs, and dog fights/ coyote attacks. This overnight shift had been no different and I was purely exhausted. It was ten am on Sunday morning (two hours passed the end of my shift) and Frank and I were finally released to clock out. She was coming back to my house for a good day's rest. At this point she had her own room and I felt like I had a grown sister in the house. We clocked out and headed toward the front desk.

We heard his voice first. "Hi. I'm here to pick up a refill for Trudy. She needs more prednisone."

I looked over at the receptionist's desk and saw a blonde-haired, blue-eyed, six-foot-plus Adonis holding a Shetland sheep dog. He looked a year or two older than us. His jeans fit perfect. His polo shirt showed off nicely sculpted biceps. Not my type but, wow. I looked over at Frank and she was standing with her mouth open and her eyes wide. He looked over and smiled at her. The attraction was instant and palpable. If it were a cartoon there would have been fireworks or birds carrying heart balloons in the air. He was the perfect Ken to her Barbie.

I looked at each of them in turn and rolled my eyes. "I'm going to walk across the street and get a cup of tea." Frank nodded but never took her eyes off of him.

I stepped out the front door and across the street to give the two of them some not-so-private privacy. Our hospital was directly across the street from an amazing little private-owned coffee shop. They knew their market. A twenty-four hour veterinary clinic where employees regularly worked more than fourteen hour shifts and clients who were upset and in need of a warm cup of comfort was at least half of their business.

I got myself a cup of chamomile and sat outside in the beautiful morning air. It had rained the day before and everything smelled clean. It was mid May so the air was cool out but the sun was warm and there wasn't a cloud to be seen. It was lovely. In the hospital, there were no windows in the treatment area and I slept during the day or was imprisoned in classrooms so I never was able to indulge in the outdoors like I had before school.

I sipped on my tea and I watched Frank, the Adonis, and the Shetland sheep dog walk out. He said something and she laughed. He got in a bright blue sports car. I remember thinking *of course he drives a sports car*. She was waiving and smiling from the front of the building as he pulled away. She looked across the street and saw me. She was half skipping and half floating across the road. She sat down and put her elbow on the table and her chin in her hand and smiled.

"What's his name?"

"Brian." She had a creepy, dreamy look on her face.

"When are you two going out?"

"Tonight!"

"Where are you going?"

"Just a little dinner" She smiled. She sighed and stretched.

"What is a guy like that doing with a sheltie?"

"It's his mother's dog!"

"So he's a mama's boy?"

"Don't you start!"

"Okay. Okay. Can we go home now? I'm, like, really tired." I yawned and drank the last of my tea.

"You're no fun!" She smacked the table as she stood up. We headed back to the car.

That night, he picked her up from my house. I was getting ready for a 6p.m. to 2a.m. shift at the data center. I had had what can only be described as a long nap thanks to Keith's incessant and loud tinkering in the garage. I was groggy and cranky when I answered the door with a coffee in my hand.

"Hello again. I'm here for Frank." He smiled and I got the first real look at his freakishly white teeth.

I stepped aside and opened the door further. "Come on in. Hey Frank!"

Keith had, of course, heard a V-8 engine pull up in front of the house and emerged from the garage to investigate. He had started putting on a few pounds at this point and his T-shirt was a little too tight. He was wiping grease from his hands with a rag when he looked up and noticed the Greek god in our living room. His face suddenly looked concerned.

"Keith, this is Brian. He's here to pick up Frank."

Keith looked a little relieved and he reached his hand out and stepped toward Brian. "Hi."

Brian's nose wrinkled a little at the greasy mitt that came towards him but he painted on a smile and shook Keith's hand. "Nice to meet you." He turned to me. "And your name is, Suzanne, right?"

"My manners. I'm sorry. Yes." I shook his hand. The way he looked in my eyes weirded me out. It was almost… predatory. "Frank! You're keeping your date waiting!"

She emerged from the hallway in a tight jeans and way too much cleavage. She was all smiles, boobs, and high heels.

He smiled at her. "Wow."

She blushed a little and picked up her purse from the floor by the door. He held out his elbow for her.

She looked over her shoulder. "I'll be back later!"

I was uneasy about the whole thing but I held up my coffee in toast to the couple. "Don't do anything I wouldn't do."

Marie Joseph-Charles 39

"That gives me plenty to do." She winked at me as she walked out the front door.

I looked at Keith. He was walking towards the living room window. "What kind of car does he drive?"

I rolled my eyes and went back towards the bedroom to finish getting ready for work.

"What?" I heard him call from the living room. "You can tell a lot about a guy by the kind of car he drives."

I turned back to face him. "What can you tell?"

"It's 4.6 liter convertible with a custom paint job. He's a total tool." I turned back towards the bedroom. "What? He probably drinks Zima!" he yelled after me.

Dinner and Disaster: By Suzanne

It was the last semester of our bachelor's. We had applied to every college of veterinary medicine in the eastern half of the United States (there were twenty) and my anxiety was ramping up in anticipation of rejection letters. Frank and I were headed back to the blue parking lot halfway across campus when suddenly she was lifted off the ground and carried about ten yards by a dark-haired assailant. It took me a moment to realize it was Ian. As soon as he set her down, she kicked him in the back of the knee and he went down like a sack of potatoes.

"OW!" He was rolling on the ground, trying to get back up. "No need to be violent."

"Serves you right! You're lucky I didn't pepper spray your ass!" She pushed her long, blonde hair out of her face.

I watched this exchange and kind of laughed. They really were like siblings.

He managed to get to his feet just as I reached them. "Here I was trying to be nice and whisk you two away to dinner!"

She looked at him with feigned anger. "I have to work at 8."

He turned to me. "You game?"

"Sure. Why not? My shift doesn't start until midnight."

We left Frank in the parking lot and walked two blocks up and one block west to the local chili hole for three ways and crackers.

It was nice to get out a little. We talked about after-college plans. He didn't really seem to have any but he still knew what he wanted to do with his life. I found that incredibly admirable. Not nearly as admirable as what he was doing for his mom, though. I couldn't honestly say I wouldn't have hired someone to care for her if I was in his position. Then again, I'm not close to my mom so I don't really have any idea what I would do.

"Where is your favorite place to hike?" He asked with half a mouthful of chilidog.

"Clifty falls."

"I haven't been there in forever! Mom likes Red River Gorge so that's where we usually did the family camping trip."

Marie Joseph-Charles 41

"I love both places. It feels like there's no one around for miles. Last time I was at Clifty, I only saw one lady and her dog the entire day."

"Did you and Keith go?"

I stifled a laugh. "I went alone. He really isn't outdoorsy."

"He wasn't that bad before he went to California. He used to skateboard all the time. I don't know what happened out there but it changed him."

"How so?"

"I think it forced him to grow up- which he needed- just not in the way he was meant to. Unnatural is the best way I can describe it."

The evening carried on and before we knew it, it was dark out. Neither of us had our phones out all through dinner and we had completely lost track of time. After we got back to campus, we said our goodbyes and went our separate ways. When I got to my car I finally looked at my phone. There were 8 missed calls and over a dozen text messages. *Where are you? What are you doing? What's for dinner? Are you okay? Are you mad at me? What's going on? Fuck you!*

I tried to call Keith back but he wouldn't answer. When I got home, he wasn't there. This was a level of mad I hadn't had to deal with from him before.

I text messaged Frank. *"Have you heard from Keith?"*

"Yeah. He called me a while ago. I told him you were eating with Ian."

"He's pissed. My phone was still on silent from class and I didn't hear it go off when he called. He left home and won't answer my calls."

"He'll get over it. He's probably at his parents' house. Give him some time to cool off."

"Okay. I'll see you at work in bit."

"See ya soon!"

Three days. It was three days before he decided to come home. I was sitting on the living room floor in my pajamas with a cup of tea and books and papers (and my cat) spread out in front of me. It was about two in the morning when I heard the door unlock.

He stepped in and looked surprised to see me. He never could keep track of my schedule.

"Hi." It was the only thing I could think to say.

"Was it good?" His face was turning red.

"Was what good?" Okay. Now I'm confused.

"Ian."

"You mean going out for chili spaghetti with a friend? Yeah, it was good."

"You expect me to believe you weren't fucking him?"

I laughed. It was the completely wrong response since he looked like he was ready to rage-cry but it just came out. I forced myself to regain composure. "Why would you think that?"

"Why wouldn't you answer your phone?"

"It was in my pocket where I always keep it."

"So you were ignoring me."

"It was on silent. I didn't even know it was going off." I could hear the pitch in my voice rising as I got angrier. "Even if I was ignoring you – which I wasn't – it would have been because I'm not rude and talk on my phone while at dinner with other people."

"You didn't look at your phone once?"

"It. Was. In. My. Pocket."

"Bullshit."

I was dumbfounded. "So you're saying the only possible explanation for me not knowing you called is that I was busy having sex with your best friend."

"Not the only one but it makes the most sense."

I was screaming in my head *oh my God! Are you serious?!* "Did you talk to Ian? Or, better yet, since you obviously don't believe the truth, go ask the manager at the restaurant for the security tapes. But make sure when you call them, you do it from your parents' house!"

I picked up my calculus book and went to bed. My cat was hot on my heals which saved him from getting hit by the slamming bedroom door.

He didn't go back to his parents' house. He slept on the couch that night. I couldn't focus to study so I closed my book and turned out the light. What just happened? What an arrogant ass.

Marie Joseph-Charles 43

How dare he? I had a nice dinner out with a friend. That's a far cry from cheating. Yes, I enjoyed Ian's company and no, I don't find him unattractive but that's still not cheating. I fell asleep angry and frustrated.

In the morning (well, later in the morning) I stumbled into the kitchen for my coffee so I could get ready for class. I must have woken him up because he came into the kitchen and wrapped his arms around me from behind. He apologized and said his old girlfriend cheated on him a lot and he guessed it made him paranoid. I thought about what Ian had said about him coming back different. He said he trusted me but he didn't trust other men (why do all men use that same bullshit line?). He promised to work on his trust issues if I paid closer attention to my phone.

I turned and looked him in the eye. "I'm going to be late for class." I grabbed my coffee and brushed past him on the way out the door.

I had never stood up for myself before. It felt good but the drive into school was plagued by fear of his retaliation.

Marie Joseph-Charles 44

The Redhead in the Library: By Ian

I was pretty pissed at Keith for accusing me of sleeping with Suzanne. She was stressed out over her vet school applications and hanging out helped take her mind off of it. I didn't see anything wrong with that. She was a really interesting person and I liked talking to her. I hardly saw him at all for like a month after that. I don't know if he was pissed at me for that long or if he was embarrassed for acting like such a dick. Knowing him, it's the first one. That guy could hold a grudge. I was afraid to call her or find her at school. I'm not sure what I was afraid of. I think I just didn't want to make her home life any more difficult.

After class I started going to the library. Mom was doing fine and told me to find something else to do and stop fussing over her. One day in fall that year I had my books spread out over a big table and I was focusing pretty hard on my laptop screen. Someone tapped me on the shoulder and scared the shit out of me.

I looked up at this cute redheaded girl who looked a year or two younger than me. "I asked 'do you mind if we share?'"

I jumped up like an idiot. "Of course. I'm sorry." I started closing the books I wasn't using and scooting things over.

She kind of giggled a little. "Thanks. I'm Megan, by the way." She set her book bag down.

I reached over the table and shook her hand. "Ian."

"Nice to meet you, Ian. Civil Engineering major."

"Oh, no. Architecture, actually."

She smiled. "I meant me."

"Oh. Right." I suddenly felt really stupid.

We studied for several more hours. I thought I heard her giggle at me when I threatened my computer. I was supposed to be creating a polyhedron with the software we were learning and only about two-thirds of the angles were working out right.

Before I knew it, a voice came over a loudspeaker and announced the library would be closing in ten minutes. Damn it.

We both stood up. She looked at me. "Same time tomorrow?"

I was kind of surprised. "Uh. Sure."

"See you tomorrow then, Architect."

Marie Joseph-Charles 45

I watched her leave as I packed up my stuff. That was a little weird.

It went on like that for like a week. I would go to the library after class and she would find me and we would share a table. Looking back on it, I was obviously oblivious. Until one day at closing time she picked up her book and looked at me. "So are you going to ask me to dinner or is this going to be the extent of our relationship?"

I felt like a deer in front of a semi. "Oh. Uh…"

"I think instead of the library we should meet at Campanello's tomorrow night. You like Italian, right?"

"Uh. Yeah."

"Good. See you tomorrow at six. Leave the books." She put her purse over her shoulder and walked out.

Wait. What?

I went home a little confused and kind of excited. I hadn't had a date in… a really long time. I calmed down quite a bit when I saw Karen's car in the driveway. What did she want? My sister and I weren't exactly friends and the thought of talking to her deflated me a lot.

I went in and set my books down by the front door. They were sitting at the kitchen table drinking coffee. Mom was smiling and looked much less pale today. Then, there was Karen. Her smile was completely fake. She was just there to make an appearance and perform her due diligence as a daughter. Disgusting. Whatever.

"Oh! Ian! Karen just brought over some baked chicken and beans. It's in the oven if you want some." My mom was smiling.

"No. I'm good."

"Oh, honey. You should eat something other than college food. You're getting thin."

"Yeah, little brother. Have some chicken." Karen pretended to smile like she cared and handed me an empty plate off the table.

"How did you mark which piece has arsenic in it?" I didn't budge from the doorway as I stared at her.

"Honestly, you two." My mom looked at each of us.

Marie Joseph-Charles 46

"I'm having Italian tomorrow. It's not college food. I have a date after school."

"Oh, honey! That's great! You haven't been on a date since high school!"

"Mom, I've been on dates. Just none of them turned into anything more."

"'Cause you're gay." My sister whispered into her mug and pretended to look out the window.

"You know what, Karen. Piss off. I didn't knock up a girl and marry her straight out of high school. Sue me. I wanted something more out of my life than a wife who's a drain like you!"

"Ian!" Mom set down her mug and stood up.

"I need a shower." I grabbed an apple off the kitchen counter and went upstairs.

I grabbed what I assumed was a clean pair of underwear out of a laundry basket in my room and locked myself in the community bathroom on the second floor. Seriously? What was her fucking problem? I'm here day in and day out. I run mom to and from her appointments, make sure she eats, paid to get what's left of her hair done so she could feel pretty… You think bringing over a half-assed dinner every once in a while makes up for it? You're a stay at home mom who pops out a kid every few years to keep from having to go back to work but you can't take time to take care of your own mother?!

My stomach growled and I remembered the apple in my hand. I turned on the shower and angrily chewed the apple while the bathroom filled with steam. I was either going to turn into a prune or boil like a lobster, but I wasn't coming out of the bathroom while *she* was still downstairs.

Companello's is a city secret. It's a family owned hole in the wall that has a great atmosphere and better food. It's down by the river so you can walk anywhere and it's the best place to get good (and real) eggplant parmesan for two on a broke college kid's budget.

I arrived at two minutes to six and parked my car in the garage across the street. Megan was standing out front waiting for me in shortish skirt (I think my mom called something like it a 'pencil skirt'). Whatever kind of skirt it was, it shaped her ass pretty nicely. I had never really noticed her appearance (aside from that ginger hair) at the library. She was in regular clothes and her hair was usually a mess with pens and pencils sticking out of it. Tonight, she was all done up with makeup and pretty hair… and that skirt. I suddenly felt like I should have put more effort into getting dressed than just a clean shirt and pants.

She saw me and smiled. "What? No flowers for your date?"

I suddenly got that deer-on-a-highway feeling again and opened my mouth to say something but she cut me off.

She was laughing. "I'm kidding. You clean up nice, Architect."

I felt so relieved that she wasn't expecting flowers that I kind of laughed a little. "You're not half bad yourself, Blatch."

"Nora Stanton Blatch Barney. She was a suffragist and civil engineer in New York in the early 1900s. I'm impressed by the reference."

"She was also an architect."

"Very true. Are we going to eat or stand out here chatting? I'm not the kind of girl who just eats salad on a first date and I skipped lunch so it may get a little ugly in there."

Okay. I liked this chick. I opened the door and motioned for her to go in first.

We were seated by a wonderful blonde woman who made me feel like I was family coming for dinner. We got a table in the corner and ordered a bottle of cheap wine. When dinner came, she wasn't kidding about things getting a little ugly. She may have been skinny but the girl could pack away some Italian food. We stayed for hours just talking about school and family and after dinner, we walked it off down by the river.

So Megan wanted to be a civil engineer to prove to her dad, who worked for the city water department, that he didn't need the son he never had. Her favorite color was sky blue. She was a Leo. Her mom was a daycare provider. I won't bore you with all of the details but I will say that she was absolutely fascinating. Some of that my have been because it had been so long since I had been on a date that went well.

At around midnight, we decided we needed to go home and get some sleep before classes the next day. I walked her to her car. This was the part that I hated. What if I leaned in for a kiss and she wasn't interested? What if I didn't try to kiss her and she got offended? What if this wasn't really a date and she thought we were just out as friends and I completely misread every signal? Jesus. I was starting to sound like Suzanne. I didn't have to worry though. When we were back at her car, she planted one right on me and even slipped me a little tongue.

"We should do this again." She reached into her purse and pulled out a piece of paper with her phone number on it. "I was thinking about sliding this across the library table to you all week but I decided that if you were a total creep, I didn't want you to have my cell number. Now that we've been out, I'm pretty sure you aren't a creep. If you had fun tonight, don't lose this." She put the paper in the palm of my hand. "See you at the library, Architect."

She got into her little silver car and drove away.

Well. That went well. Not at all how I expected. But well. I went back to my car in the garage around the corner and drove home smiling like I just had my first kiss. I saved her number in my phone before I went to bed and hid the paper she had given me in a dresser drawer.

Meeting Megan: by Suzanne

We had all come together to celebrate Brian's birthday. I
still didn't care for him, but Frank was head over heals. Frank,
Brian, Keith, and I were already seated at the restaurant when Ian
and a red-headed girl arrived.

He stood at the end of our table. "Guys, this is Megan.
Megan, this is Keith, Suzanne, Frank, and birthday boy Brian." He
pointed to each of us in turn.

"It's nice to meet you all." She smiled and waived at us all.

I stood and shook her hand. "Nice to meet you too."

She and Ian sat in the remaining chairs. She talked to us all
as if she knew us. It was kind of nice that she didn't feel like an
outsider. She even sang loud and proud when they brought out a
flaming cupcake and we sang Happy Birthday to Brian.

Okay. So here's the deal. Don't get me wrong. I liked
Megan well enough as a person. She was smart and had a great
sense of humor. She had big eyes and pointed chin but she was
lean and pretty. Overall, she was the halfway point between
Frank's beautiful, bubbly perfection and my subtlety and
sullenness. The problem was, over the years, I would get
progressively worsening negative feelings whenever I saw her and
Ian together. I always managed to shake it off or set it aside and I
never let it show. Like I said, I liked her and I liked seeing Ian
happy but it just didn't feel right.

Bridge Tour: by Ian

It was around March or April in '08. I wanted to do something nice for Megan. She and I had been dating for a while and it felt like our whole relationship was dinner or studying and going back to her place for… other stuff. I really liked her and I wanted her to understand that I felt like there should be more depth to our relationship. Now that I've said that out loud, I feel like a woman. Anyways. I wasn't quite sure how to handle it. What else is there to dating besides those three things?

I tried asking Frank but her response was, 'you know her better than I do!' That wasn't helpful at all. I was looking for a basic woman's perspective.

I called Suzanne. "I need help."

"No kidding."

"I'm being serious. I want to do something special for Megan."

"Take her to a nice dinner."

"That's not special. That's fancy normal."

"What does she like?"

"Basketball and nachos."

"You don't have any more insight than that."

I thought about it. "Not really."

"Ugh. You're such a guy."

"What's that supposed to mean?"

"What is she passionate about? And not in the bedroom."

I thought harder. "School, I guess."

"And what is she going to school for?"

"City planning.

"Keep thinking."

I hate women's games. Just tell me. "I can take her to city hall."

"That'd be funny. She'll think you're there to get married."

Oops. Nix that idea. "Never mind that."

"Okay, Romeo. Clearly this is too difficult for you. My dad works closely with the historical society. If you're nice to me, I'll get you guys tickets for the tour they're doing of all of the bridges."

Marie Joseph-Charles 51

"Why? We drive over those bridges every day."

She sighed loudly. "Don't bridges connecting the two states have a major impact on traffic and tourism. You know... *the city.*"

"Yeah."

"Okay, clearly you need this spelled out. She is going to school for city planning. You are going for architecture. I am offering you a tour of the historical impact of BOTH of those things and I'm pretty sure I'm doing it about the time you are supposed to be working on term papers."

I felt like someone suddenly turned on a light bulb in my brain. It was genius. No way was I giving Suzanne the credit if this went well.

As if she could hear the light come on, I heard laughing on the other end of the line. "I take it that's a 'yes?'"

I felt a little stupid. "Yes, please."

"Tour starts at the Cincinnati side of the Purple People Bridge at 1pm Saturday. I'll have the tickets for you on Wednesday."

"Thank you. I owe you."

"Oh, yes. Yes, you do. And I will collect or I'll rat you out to Megan. Don't think I don't know you're planning on taking the credit for this."

"That's blackmail."

"That's leverage, Love. See you Wednesday."

I set my phone down on the arm of the chair. Women are so manipulative. She was right, of course. But, still. It was pretty fucking brilliant; I do have to give her that.

Saturday was amazing. We hit them all: The Purple People Bridge, The Roebling Suspension Bridge, the Clay Wade Bailey Bridge, and the Taylor Southgate Bridge. I'm not much of a history person, but it was actually pretty cool. Megan was frantically scribbling notes and smiling so hard, I thought her face would crack. We had chili spaghetti for lunch and ended with ice cream and a stroll back across the Purple People Bridge to the car.

"This could not have possibly been a better day!" I had my arm around her and she leaned into my chest.

"Well, good. You planning on publishing those notes? You took enough to write a book."

"This has given me a great idea for my paper. I wanted to make sure I got enough of the details before I go to the library and research on my own."

"I'm going to need to borrow your notes."

She laughed and licked her ice cream. "I figured. Whose idea was it?"

"Whose idea was what?"

"This little adventure. You're sweet, Architect, but not really the kind that would come up with something like this on your own."

"I'm hurt!" I backed away from her and grabbed my chest.

"Wouldn't be Frank. She'd enjoy watching you squirm coming up with ideas on your own and well, let's face it, Keith is about as romantic as a plague-infested rat." She smiled. "I'll have to tell Suzanne, 'thank you.'"

My cover was blown. "At least she won't be able to blackmail me now."

She laughed. "I doubt it was blackmail. Probably just a little leverage."

2am Milkshakes: Suzanne

Gearing up for the next phase in my life was exhausting. I had gotten accepted to Ohio State University veterinary program but Frank was going to Purdue. She was moving three hours into Indiana and I was trying to work out school, commuting, work, and survival.

It was about 2:30 in the morning when I awoke from a dead sleep. Without moving I took a deep breath. "What do you want?" I opened my eyes. Frank was kneeling next to the bed, staring at me.

"I need a milkshake."

"Let me get dressed."

She left the room and I rolled over and looked at Keith. I swore that man could sleep through a nuclear bomb. A potential intruder just entered our home and came into our bedroom and he didn't even twitch. I rolled over and pulled on the first pair of pants and shirt I came across, hoping they were clean enough to go out in public. I stumbled into the living room in my flip-flops. It was May and kind of cold out, but I was too tired to care.

She was barely seated on the couch and almost bouncing. "I'm driving!"

For quite some time it was our ritual to go to the twenty-four-hour burger and shake joint by my house whenever one of us had something important to talk about. We seated ourselves. She ordered a peanut butter and chocolate chip shake. I had my standard vanilla.

"Okay. What's so important that I don't get to sleep?"

She looked at me. "How did you know Keith was the one?"

"The one what?"

"Like, how did you know you wanted to spend your life with Keith?"

"I don't know. Not for sure anyway."

"You live with him and you don't know if you want to spend the rest of your life with him?"

"No. Not at all. I think it's ignorant to believe that I'm going to meet the person I'm doomed to grow old with this early in my life. As we get older, we change so it makes sense that the person we are with might change too. There's a possibility that there is one person for someone through every stage in their life. I look at my grandparents as an example. But I don't think it's necessarily for everyone."

Frank looked down at her shake and stirred slowly with the straw. "Do you think Wes might have something to do with that belief?"

I kind of laughed a little. "Wes didn't change. I blinded myself to the person he really was throughout our entire relationship. When I took off the rose-colored glasses and saw him for the waste of space he was, I was free to find someone who could make me happy."

"That makes sense. In a way, you were the one who changed by realizing what was going on." She took a sip of her shake.

"Yeah. I guess so. Why are you asking about me and Keith anyway?"

"Well. I just don't know."

I leaned back in the booth and took a deep breath. "You don't know what?"

"Well. I just don't know how I feel about Brian."

"What do you mean you don't know how you feel about Brian? Normally the only way to get you two apart is with a crowbar."

"Well. I really like him."

"And?'

"No. I mean I *really* like him. I'm awake at three o'clock in the morning because I can't stop thinking about how happy he makes me."

"Okay… So what's the question?"

"He's willing to move to Indiana with me."

"That still doesn't answer *my* question."

"Are we at a point in our relationship where we can not only live together, but move out of state together? Away from our family and friends and just be us?"

"You are answering a question with a question. At any rate, I don't think there's a set timeline that fits every relationship.

Marie Joseph-Charles 55

If you're comfortable with him and you trust him and he is willing to move three hours away so that he can be with you, I don't see what the problem is."

"Well what if he moves and it doesn't work?"

"Then he moves back and you keep going to school."

"What if I need his income?"

"Don't ever let yourself get into a position where you are reliant on someone else's income. Yes, Keith moved in with me to help me with bills but I was surviving before him and- believe it or not- I can survive if he were to leave tomorrow. I may be living off of Ramen and toast, but I can survive."

She looked back down at her shake. "I guess that makes sense. I don't know. I've never lived with someone else before. Other than like my parents and kind of you part time."

I laughed. "That's a little different. You guys need to sit down and hash out certain rules and policies for you both to follow."

"Like what?"

"Like who is going to be responsible for most dinners? Are you going to be expected to cook and clean all the time while you're in school? I'm pretty sure that's not going to work."

"That's fair."

"Who's going to be responsible for laundry? If you're renting a house, who's going to be in charge of the yard work? You guys need to work out who is going to be responsible for what, especially when it comes to bills. You want to make sure everything gets paid on time. Will both your names be on them all or will your name only be on the ones you're responsible for? Will you have a joint bank account or give each other cash if you both chip in for something like groceries?"

"Is this what you and Keith did before he moved in?"

"No. That's why I'm telling you to make sure you do it. Learn from my mistakes. It will save you a lot of arguments later."

She kind of laughed. "I can respect that."

A play: Ian

I really liked Megan. She was a lot of fun. We had a lot in common and since our majors were on the same track, we could help each other study (instead of just sitting in the library at the same table). We both liked action movies with a lot of explosions and Chinese food. It was kind of hard to find time together though. She was on scholarship but she had to work a part time job to afford the basics. I was always busy. During the week was packed with classes, studying, and taking care of the house and my mom. Weekends were for work. Two fourteen to sixteen hour days (depending on the time of year) back to back was exhausting so I really didn't have time for her on the weekends either.

One day, we were going into the library and saw one of the drama nerds hanging a poster for the new play.

"Cool! They're doing The Tempest! It's about time they picked a decent Shakespeare play. I swear it's like people think the only play he ever wrote was Romeo and Juliet. Want to go?"

"To a college rendition of Shakespeare? No thank you."

"Why not? The Tempest is, like, the best play he ever wrote. An evil king, revenge plot, coup de tat, romance…" I nudged her with my elbow.

"Yeah. I'm not good at following old English and plays seriously bore me."

Okay. We had a lot in common but not everything. "Okay. Fine."

"Hey. I didn't say you can't go. I just won't be going with you."

"I have your permission then?" I was being little sarcastic.

"If it keeps me from feeling guilty about not going, yes."

I took one of the pamphlets the kid had hung with the flyers. "Well, okay then."

After we left the library for the evening, I was heading back to my house and made a detour passed Keith and Suzanne's house. Keith had said he needed me to look at something he was drawing up. He couldn't find a hood he could afford and was thinking about fiberglassing one for now. I don't know how he thought I could help him replicate a hood for a '67 Corvair without one to go

off of. I think he just needed to talk it out with someone and
Suzanne was stiffing him to study. I knocked on the door and
Suzanne opened it.

She smiled. "When are you going to stop knocking and
just come in?"

"I don't want to walk in on something I'd rather not see."

"No worries about that." She said it kind of under her
breath.

Keith was sitting on the couch in a pair of flannel pants and
no shirt. He'd put on quite a bit of weight and he was a really
fucking hairy guy. He kind of looked like a gorilla in pajamas. He
was typing away on his laptop.

Without even looking up from the screen he moved the
pillow he was resting his arm on. "Come here and look at this."

I set my book bag down by the door and sat on the couch
next to him. Suzanne was sitting on the floor with open books and
note cards in a circle around her. I half listened to Keith explain
his dilemma. Since I was only half listening I don't remember
most of the conversation. The other half of me was focused on
Suzanne and watching her study technique. She had an egg timer
with her set for fifteen minutes. She had four clusters of books and
notes arranged in a circle around her. Every fifteen minutes she
would rotate to a different book and take notes. When she made a
full rotation, it was an hour and she got up and walked around and
changed laundry or loaded the dishwasher. She did this for a
couple of hours I was there.

When we had hashed out Keith's problem, I picked up my
book bag and the pamphlet for the play fell out. Suzanne picked it
up.

She looked really excited. "They're doing The Tempest?
No way!"

I took the pamphlet back from her. "You like that play?"

"You're joking, right? You never wondered why my *male*
cat is named Ariel?"

Keith looked up from the computer. "The cat's a guy? I
just thought you liked The Little Mermaid."

I looked at him kind of incredulously. "Dude. Even I
knew the cat was male." I looked back down at Suzanne. She was

looking at him sort of in disbelief but sort of saying 'are you an idiot?' "You want to go? I do still owe you for that bridge tour thing."

She turned back towards me. "I'd love to! But I don't know if I can get off work."

"You need a break." I pointed to her books all over the floor. "And they are doing a couple of Thursday shows. It's going on the whole month of October. I'm sure you can find *a day*."

Keith piped up. "What about me?"

I looked at him. "Do you want to go?"

"Not really, but I'd like to be invited."

"Dude, I've known you for over a decade. I'm not going to waste my breath inviting you to something I know you have absolutely no interest in."

He looked a little irritated. "Fine."

I looked back at Suzanne. "What do you think?"

She looked around at her books. "Maybe you're right."

Suzanne was able to switch a shift with someone at the vet place on a Saturday night. I was pretty excited. I put on nice pants and a clean shirt and dug my church shoes out of the back of the closet. It was only a college play but you're supposed to dress up for the theater, right?

I went downstairs and kissed my mom's forehead. She'd been looking a little pale and I was kind of worried about leaving her alone.

She looked me up and down. "Look at my boy. All grown up and handsome. Where are you taking Megan, all dressed up like that?"

"I'm going to a play but Megan didn't want to go so I'm going with Suzanne."

"Suzanne? She's the one that makes that bread I like?"

"That's her."

She suddenly looked kind of serious. "You're not dating two women, are you?"

"Mom. No. Suzanne is a good friend who likes the same play I do."

She kind of squinted at me. "Okay, then. Have fun."

Marie Joseph-Charles 59

When I picked Suzanne up, it kind of felt like picking up a date from her parents' house. I still remember how she looked when she came out of the bedroom. I'd never really seen her all dressed up before. It was a short black dress that had folds in the front and draped over her neck. She had in silver ear rings and she was wearing makeup. I may have been staring a little. She looked totally different- not that she usually looked bad- but *damn!* Keith looked a lot like an over protective dad until he kissed her goodbye. He looked me right in the eye, gave her a really over-the-top kiss and looked at me again. I got the feeling he was marking his territory. Whatever.

The ride to campus was kind of nice. We got caught up on what was going on with school. Since she had to drive to Columbus every day now, I didn't really see much of her.

"The thing I miss most is sunlight." She was looking down at her hands in her lap.

"What do you mean?"

"I get up before the sun and come home after dark. If I come home at all. Sometimes I sleep in my car at the truck stop. I work in windowless rooms on the weekends."

I felt bad for her. At least I got to work outside. I told her when she graduated I'd take her to Clifty Falls to celebrate.

When we got to campus, she made me escort her properly. It felt a little weird when she took my arm. I know we were good friends but there was this little nagging piece of me that felt a little more.

We were sitting practically on top of each other. The school theater was old and cramped. I didn't mind though. She smelled like lavender. I kept glancing over at her through the play. I could see the little crinkles in her eyes when she laughed. It was far more entertaining to watch her reactions than the play itself. The kid they got to play Prospero was awful. At least the bar afterwards was fun.

Marie Joseph-Charles 60

A Night Out: By Suzanne

I was so excited about going to the play. I owed Bethany BIG TIME for switching shifts with me. It was going to completely upset the balance of my sleep schedule but at the time, I didn't care.

That night, I showered, shaved, waxed, and plucked. I think the last time I put that much effort into my appearance was when I was a teenager. Maybe prom? I had gone out and bought makeup just for the night. I hated the stuff. I touch my face a lot so I mess it up and I sweat at work so it runs. Nail polish? Please. I handle poop, blood, and pee for a living. When I heard Ian's voice in the living room, I felt kind of electrified. This was really happening! I was going *out!* I did one last check in the mirror. I had only barely painted my face, but it was enough to make me scared I had screwed it up.

When I walked into the living room, Ian looked genuinely surprised. I'm not sure if it was because I actually looked like a girl or if it was because I had kind of over dressed. He, however, looked… wow. His hair was actually combed. His red shirt made his eyes look darker. I loved his eyes. His pants were actually clean and his belt wasn't frayed. It was a far cry from the Ian I was used to seeing, but I wasn't complaining.

Keith's ridiculous kiss kind of made me mad. We had had a long talk about how this wasn't a date and he didn't need to feel threatened, especially by his best friend. It didn't matter. He had some pretty big insecurities about the whole thing. I wish I'd known that night just how bad they were going to get.

On the way to campus, Ian and I tried to get caught up a little. I confessed that my crazy schedule was already causing me to be a little depressed. The days were getting shorter and I was very much an outdoor kind of girl. But, with school taking up my whole days and studying taking up my nights, the most fresh air I got was walking to class.

"Well, I'll tell you what," he smiled at me, "when you graduate, I will take you to Clifty Falls to celebrate."

My heart kind of lifted. "You promise?"

"Scout's honor."

Marie Joseph-Charles 61

"I didn't know you were a scout."

"I wasn't, but I still mean it." He kind of smirked.

He had a cute smirk.

When we pulled into the parking lot and got out of the car, I put my arm through his and held his bicep… his firm, very prevalent bicep…

"What's this?" he looked over at me.

"I put on a dress and painted my face. I'm going full girl tonight so you are going to escort this lady like a gentleman."

He smiled. I love that smile. I felt some fluttering in my stomach.

When we entered the auditorium, some of the cast members were in full costume in the lobby to greet guests. Someone had put out a rumor that a scout from one of the bigger acting troupes in the area was going to be in attendance. I recognized Prospero immediately.

"Oh my God! Suz!" Robbie ran up and gave me a hug.

I let go of Ian's arm and hugged him back. "Robbie! How have you been? I didn't even know you went to school here!"

"I just transferred. Better opportunities, ya know?" He looked at Ian. "And you are?"

Ian held out his hand and shook Robbie's. "Ian. Ian Riker."

"I'm Rob Outt. Suz and I go back a ways." He let go of Ian's hand and smiled at me. "You're a lucky guy, Ian. I tried to get this girl to go on a date with me for four years."

Ian opened his mouth, but I interjected. "We aren't on a date. Ian and I are just friends."

"Really? Does that mean I'd have a shot now?" He stepped in front of Ian.

"Nope. Curtain is in fifteen. You might want to take your place." I stepped around him and put my arm back through Ian's.

As we walked towards our seats, I heard Robbie shout "Lucky guy, Ian!"

"What was that all about?" Ian pulled my arm closer to him.

"Robbie and I went to high school together. We were both kind of outcasts. He was friends with Wes and constantly tried to get me to leave him. He was relentless."

"Do I need to go back and beat him up?"

I kind of smiled. "I can handle Robbie."

The play itself wasn't the best performance but I didn't care. I was out. There were a few flubs and mishaps on stage that were kind of funny. The string holding the moon broke and the balloon gently wafted towards the audience. That was pretty hilarious. All night I kept feeling like there I was being watched, but Robbie couldn't see me from the stage and when I would glancc over at Ian, he was always facing forward. I was afraid he could hear my stomach. I had forgotten to eat again and I felt like it was drowning out the actors.

At the conclusion, we all stood and applauded. Ian stopped clapping when Robbie returned to the stage but resumed when the girl playing Miranda stepped out. I felt that was a little childish of him, but Robbie was kind a bad actor.

When the applause concluded and the house lights came back on, Ian held his arm back out for me. "Come on. Let's get you something to eat."

I was a little embarrassed. "You could hear that, huh?"

"I'm pretty sure the guy up in the technical booth could hear you."

I felt like I was blushing.

Ian took me to a little bar near campus and ordered me a glass a wine and a beer for him. We split an appetizer sampler and laughed about how bad the play was. It had been a while since I'd had that much fun.

It was late when I got home. Keith was sitting on the couch in his bathrobe. "Have fun?"

"Yes! The play was awful, I loved it!"

"That makes no sense."

"I know!" I couldn't stop grinning.

"How was dinner after?"

"We didn't really have dinner. We just split an appetizer over drinks. It was nice."

"You didn't tell me you were going to Vino's after."

Marie Joseph-Charles 63

I stopped smiling. "I didn't say where we went."

"I know. My coworker, Curtis, saw you there and text me that you were cheating on me."

"Did you set him straight?"

"He sent me this." He tossed his phone at me.

I looked at it. It was a picture of Ian and me sitting at the bar. We were laughing. "That's a good picture."

"That's all you have to say?" He stood up.

"What are you wanting me to say?"

"I don't know. I don't like the way you two are looking at each other, though."

"Are you kidding?"

"No."

I rolled my eyes and tried to walk back to the bedroom. He grabbed my arm. I turned. "What?!"

He let go. I went back to the bedroom and slammed the door.

Thanksgiving '08: by Suzanne

Frank and Brian had waived goodbye to Cincinnati in July. They'd found a little house to rent near the school and Brian had found a job quickly. They wanted to get settled in completely before Frank's fall classes started. When their moving truck was loaded, there were a lot of tears (mostly from Frank's parents, Steve and Cathy). They promised to keep in touch and we kept reminding each other that it was only three hours away.

The first Thanksgiving of vet school, Frank had somehow conned us all into driving three hours into Indiana. It was actually the weekend after thanksgiving and she had insisted that we all come out and stay so that we could have Friendsgiving followed by our own fake Black Friday girl's shopping day. She was dying to have her first big holiday in the little house that she and Brian had found to rent. For as long as I had known her, Frank was a bad ass blonde bombshell with a Suzy Homemaker core. She had always wanted to do the whole happily-married-with-kids bit and this was her first step. How could we deny her? Better question: How could we deny her and expect to live? I have no doubt she would have driven to Cincinnati, clubbed us in our sleep, and dragged us out there.

Keith and I took my car (it got better gas mileage) and Ian and Megan took her car in case she had to "leave his ass in the middle of nowhere." She and Ian had been dating for over a year but she still felt pretty new to our group.

I wish I had ridden with the other two. Keith could have taken himself out there. For three hours I had to listen to him complain that the drive was so long and the view was so boring. We were from Ohio. I had a two hour commute to and from school if I came home. Cornfields and open landscape were the same no matter what state. At least he seemed excited to see Frank.

There were apartments near campus back home that were bigger than this house. At one story and two bedrooms, it had to have been barely eight hundred square feet. Despite the size, I could see why Frank picked it. The neighborhood didn't look too bad. It was white siding with blue trim and shutters. It had a matching, albeit slightly rundown, detached garage in the back. But the crème was the white picket fence. It was a little storybook home that fit perfectly into Frank's fantasy.

I had barely shut off the car when Frank came busting out the front door in a tea length dress and kitchen apron. Her hair was a little disheveled and there was flour on her apron but otherwise, she was the perfect picture of a stereotypical housewife. I'd never seen her smile so wide. She hugged us each in turn and then shooed the men out to the garage while partially dragging Megan and me into the house.

She gave us a short tour (there really wasn't a way to make a tour in a house that small last very long) that ended in the kitchen. She had the table made for six. She must have spent DAYS copying centerpieces, homemade napkin holders, a cornucopia, and even a leaf-rubbing tablecloth from just about every magazine she could get her hands on.

"Wow." Megan was clearly awestruck by Frank's efforts.

I, on the other hand, wasn't surprised by the table. What got me was when I looked at the little half-wall that separated the kitchen from the living room. "Holy Hell, Frank. How many pies did you make?"

She giggled. "I wanted to make sure everyone felt at home. My favorite is pecan, Brian likes cherry, you like pumpkin, Keith's is chocolate mousse, Ian's is turtle," she turned to Megan "and Ian said you like apple but he couldn't be more specific so I made regular and caramel apple."

Megan's face flushed and her cheeks almost matched her red hair. "You didn't have to go to so much effort for me."

"Nonesense!" Frank put her arm around Megan. "Ian likes you. You're as good as family."

Megan smiled. Frank really knew how to make someone feel welcome.

I looked back at the stove. Turkey in the oven, salad on the counter, wine in a chiller, corn, mashed potatoes, two kinds of gravy… "Frank, did you get up at like two this morning to do all of this."

She threw her head back and laughed. "You're assuming I ever went to bed!"

Megan and I just stood and stared at her.

Megan finally stepped forward. "What can we do to help?"

Frank's smile got so big her face could have cracked. "Grab that wooden spoon and start stirring that white gravy so it doesn't get lumpy. Suzanne, crack a bottle of wine. We need a drink!"

We spent the next hour in the kitchen getting tipsy, talking about school, and just a dash of man bashing. I hadn't had that much fun in a long time.

"I think that about does it!" Frank was so pleased as she set the last serving bowl on the table. She grabbed a walkie talkie off the window sill. "Dinner is served!"

Brian's voice came back through. "We'll be in in a minute, Hun."

Frank was beaming. "I need to go freshen up!" She disappeared into the bathroom. It seemed like she was only gone for about two minutes before she re-emerged with her makeup flawless and her hair up in a perfect bun.

We sat around the table. I remember thinking, *Please don't make us say what we are thankful for.*

She turned to Brian. "Say grace?"

I was a little surprised but that, but okay. We each held hands and lowered our heads.

Brian cleared his throat. "Thank you, Lord, for this wonderful meal. We ask that you keep those who are not so fortunate as to have food tonight in your heart and provide for them. We thank you for allowing us to be together to share this and for blessing my beautiful girlfriend with such amazing culinary skills." He looked up at her and smiled. "Amen."

We all followed, "Amen." I had to admit that even though I really didn't like Brian, he was good to Frank.

Halfway through dinner I decided I wanted more vegetables. I looked at Ian. "Will you pass the broccoli?"

"Woah, Babe. You might want to slow down. You're not eating for two." Now, there's the Keith that liked to come out around other people. The asshole who belittled me to feel macho.

Everyone seemed to stop and look at him.

Ian froze with the bowl of broccoli still in the air. "Dude. Really?"

"She knows I'm just joking." He nudged me with his elbow.

I took the bowl from Ian and half-heartedly put a spoonful on my plate.

After dinner, we all helped clean. Keith and Brian were arguing some football nonsense and Frank was giving a Megan a tutorial on how she had made the origami turkey napkin rings. I quietly slipped out the front door for a little air. I hadn't been as discrete as I thought; Ian came out shortly behind me.

He sat down on the porch swing next to me. "You okay?"

"Yeah. Just needed a little air. I didn't hear how your Thanksgiving with your family went."

He looked out over the front lawn. "Not much to tell. Me and Mom cooked a big dinner for us because my stupid sister and her family were supposed to come eat but they decided to eat at their house and come after so we'll be eating leftovers 'til Christmas."

I turned to him. "I've never heard you say anything nice about your sister. You really hate each other?"

"Yup. Since childhood.'

"Why? I don't have any living siblings so I'm sorry if I'm prying, but I don't understand."

"When my dad left, she convinced me it was my fault. She said I had broken the family and it would never be fixed."

"Wow. Why would she say something like that?"

"Uncle Pete said it's because I was the favorite. I was the 'good kid' and she was jealous and she was lashing out. But it stuck even twenty years later."

"If you don't mind my asking, why did your dad really leave?"

"Mom said at the end of the day, they were better friends than lovers. Aunt Leena said he had another family that Mom didn't know about. Uncle Pete says he was too immature for a family and freaked out. That's why he never contacted us afterwards. I think that one's the most likely. Truthfully, I stopped caring why."

"Do you hate him?"

"I used to. But how do you hate someone you barely remember? What about you? I never hear you talk about your mom."

I looked down at the pop can that Keith had been using to put his cigarettes out. "I cut ties with Angela a long time ago."

"Fair enough."

We sat outside and looked at the stars until it got too chilly and we were forced to go back in.

Different Nuts from the Same Tree: By Ian

The morning after that big Thanksgiving dinner, Frank had us all up at SIX IN THE FUCKING MORNING. What kind of monster does that to guests? The four of us were in the study room/spare bedroom. Brian said the couch pulled out into a twin bed if we wanted to flip for it but we all agreed to just sleep on the floor. I honestly don't think any couple could have fit on it anyway. Me and Megan were sleeping perfectly well next to the wall while Suzanne and Keith were on the other side of the room under the window. When Frank decided it was time to get up, she cracked me in the head with the door. HARD.

"Ow! Son of a bitch!" I rolled over almost on top of Megan and grabbed for my head.

"Sorry! Us girls have shopping to do and there's a day of male bonding planned for you! Breakfast will be ready in ten." She was all sunshine and smiles when she shut the door. Total fucking monster.

I looked at Megan. She smiled. "That's going to leave a mark."

"Is that why you wanted to sleep on my left this time?"

Her smile got bigger. "Maybe. I didn't think you would be dumb enough to sleep with your head that close to the door on purpose."

"Thanks." I kissed her and she laughed.

I sat up. My head really hurt. I looked over at Suzanne and Keith. Suz was sitting up and rubbing her eyes. About four feet away, Keith was snoring loudly.

"Is that him making that noise?" Megan's eyes got wide.

"Yeah. We forgot his CPAP." Suzanne stretched and cracked her neck.

"Jesus. At least you'll know if he dies in his sleep."

"Not if the machine's on. It basically breathes for him."

"How did he sleep through this one yelling?" She chucked a thumb at me.

"He can sleep through anything. I wish I was exaggerating. And he won't be functional until he's had at least five hundred milligrams of caffeine but he's typically had at least eight hundred before lunch."

Megan's eyes looked like they might pop out of her head. "That can't be healthy."

"Nope. He knows it too. He just doesn't care." She slid over to him and pulled the blankets off of him. "Cold feet usually works." She slid her feet under his shirt and pushed them against his back.

"Fuck! What the fuck?" he moved away from her but his yes were still closed.

"Everyone is waiting on you! Wake up!" She was yelling only a few feet from his face. She looked at Megan and me. "Four… Three… Two…"

As if on cue, he started snoring again. She put her feet back on him. "Fuck! Quit it! I'm awake!"

"No you aren't. Get up!" She was rocking him with her legs until he finally rolled over on his own and sat up.

"Do you have to do that every morning?" Megan was half giggling but looked kind of concerned.

"No. I'm not usually home. That's why he's usually late for work."

"I'm not that bad." Keith was yawning and rubbing his face.

The door started to swing open again but this time I was able to dive out of the way. The girls were laughing and falling over.

"Coffee!" Frank announced and shut the door again.

"She's like a demon cuckoo clock from Hell." I rubbed where she hit me earlier. Megan kissed my head and helped pull me up.

We stumbled into the living room and to the kitchen. Frank had six mugs of coffee ready with cream and sugar on the table. There was fruit, fried potatoes, pancakes, bacon, and a giant bowl of scrambled eggs too. Frank really knew how to go all out. We each took our place at the table while she and Brian laid out the game plan for the day. After breakfast, we each took our turns in the shower while we continued to caffeinate. By nine, we all somewhat resembled functioning adults. Frank shooed the girls out the door and left me, Brian, and Keith in the kitchen with the third pot of coffee.

Keith turned to Brian. "So we finally get to meet the other Calloway men?"

Brian took a deep breath. "Yeah."

"Frank said your brothers were coming over. How many do you have?" I poured myself a third- maybe fourth- cup of coffee.

"Four. I'm the youngest."

"Damn. Are you full siblings?" Keith's looked amazed.

"Yeah. Five boys. No girls."

"Your poor mother." I was kind of joking.

"Granddad always said that 'a wife's duties are too look right, care for the family, and bear sons.' Mom did all of those dutifully."

Um. Granddad said it, but did Brian believe it? Before I could ask, the door burst open and four of the biggest men I had ever seen in my life came in. Brian and I were both over six foot and all four of these guys towered over us. They all had sandy or blonde hair and light eyes. They were all heavily muscled, physically fit like Brian, and wore tight sweaters to show it off. I felt horribly inadequate.

"Hey Tater Tot!" The biggest one almost lifted Brian out of his chair and gave him a hug.

Keith spit out a little of his coffee. "Tater tot?"

If looks could kill…

Brian hugged each one of them and then turned to face us at the table. "This is Ian and Keith."

I half-waved. "Howdy."

Keith raised his mug like a toast.

"These are my brothers Rob, Trevor, Dylan, and Zack." He pointed to each one as he said his name. It looked like they were all close in age so figuring out who was older than who was almost impossible.

"Did your mother have a cloning machine?" Keith finally set his mug down.

"Lots of nuts from the same tree." The one called Zack put his arms around the two closest brothers.

Rob, the biggest one that had pulled Brian up, spoke up. "49-ers game tonight?"

"Hell, no! My house. My rules. Steelers/Patriots or you can go home." Brian crossed his arms.

"Fine." Rob clapped him on the back hard enough to push him forward a little. "We kicking your ass in the yard or the park this time?"

I looked at him. "This time?"

"Annual Calloway Thanksgiving Day game! Three on three. It's tradition. Show them what happened when you didn't move fast enough last week."

Brian looked annoyed. He lifted the left side of his shirt. On his ribs was a HUGE skull-shaped purple and yellow bruise.

"Are you fit to play today?" I was a little concerned. It looked like he may have a cracked rib or something.

"Of course!" He looked at his brothers like he was daring them to challenge him. "I already scoped out that Cumberland park on the corner N Salisbury and Kalberer for us."

"Shotgun!" Trevor ran out the front door.

Dylan rolled his eyes. "Fucking idiot has the keys! All the looks. None of the brains." He went out the front door.

All the looks? You all look alike!

"Guess we'll see you there, Tater!" Rob ruffled Brian's hair and left with Zack.

Brian took a deep breath after they left. "Do either of you have brothers?"

"Nope. Fucking useless sister but that's it." I stood up.

"I've got a step brother but he lives in Mexico or Monaco or somewhere that starts with an 'M'."

Brian tried to fix his hair in the reflection of the microwave. "You are both very, very lucky."

At the park, we split three on three. Rob, Trevor and Zack versus me, Brian and Keith.

Keith looked at Dylan. "You don't play?"

Dylan smiled. "Once upon a time. Have to settle as ref now." He lifted up his right pants leg and showed off a shiny stainless steel calf. "Cut off by a jaw trap set by poachers while I was hiking. Had to use my belt as a tourniquet to stop the

bleeding. Thankfully I was only about 12 miles from base camp.
I'm still the best cop on the force though!"

I looked at Brian. No way that was true. He nodded to me.
He was getting ready to play full contact football with cracked – if
not broken- ribs. His brother lost his leg to a bear trap in the
mountains and is still an active police officer. Who the fuck were
these guys?

That was one of the most brutal games I have ever played
in my life. I played basketball in high school so I was quick and
could turn on a dime, but these guys could predict almost
everything I did! Trevor made the mistake of trying to takedown
tackle Keith. Keith was a brick wall. He was short, wide, and
getting overweight. Trevor was muscular but lean and tall. He had
no chance. The most action I saw from Keith was when he scored
a touchdown. He spiked the ball and lit a celebratory cigarette
right there in the end zone. At one point, Rob sent Brian airborne
and Zack came at him from the other direction and I swear to God
he spun in the air! These guys were out for blood.

I was never more grateful for a game to end! I don't
remember the score but we didn't even come CLOSE to winning.
We were bruised, battered, and I'm pretty sure Brian was broken
again. Keith seemed to come out of it the least scathed. The Killer
Clan piled into the pickup and said they'd meet us at the house.

I turned to Brian. "Are all your games like that?"

"They went easy on us. Rob said earlier that they could
snap you in half and Keith is clearly out of shape so it wasn't going
to be a fair fight. You should see when it's three Calloways
against three Calloways. There's usually a trip to the hospital on
Thanksgiving or Christmas." We got into Brian's little blue sports
car and headed back to the house.

When we got there, the girls were already home. I could
see the MOUNTAIN of shopping bags in the back window of
Megan's car. Oh, goodie. Brian's brothers had parked their truck
in the driveway behind Frank's car so Brian cussed under his
breath when he parked his car on the street. We went inside; well,
Brian and I went in while Keith stayed on the porch for a cigarette.
It's a good thing he did too. The first thing I saw was Zack
holding Suzanne's hand and her laughing. I'm not sure what he

was doing but if Keith had seen it, there would have been the trip to the hospital Brian was talking about.

Suzanne looked up from Zack and saw us before Megan (who was pouring chips into a bowl and talking to Rob) or Frank (who was plating up chicken wings). "Oh, my God! Are you guys okay?" She let go of Zack's hand.

Frank and Megan looked up. "Jesus! Honey!" Megan ran up to me. She kissed me and it hurt. Apparently, my lip was split.

Frank put her hand on Brian's face. "I thought you told me you wouldn't play to rough." She was pissed but concerned.

"It's not as bad as it looks. I promise." He kissed her hand.

"We'll talk about it later." She turned back to the kitchen.

Brian looked over at Rob on the sofa. Rob mouthed *somebody's in trouble.* Brian flipped him off.

Keith came in. "What did I miss?"

Suzanne was still in the kitchen. She looked at him. "You okay?"

"Why wouldn't I be?"

Trevor was sitting at the table next to the refrigerator and stuffing chips in his mouth. "Your man's a fucking tank." He looked at Suz.

She sighed and grabbed a can of pop from the ice chest behind her. She brought it to Keith.

He took it from her. "Thank you."

Rob piped up. "There is beer, though, right?"

We all gathered in the living room to watch the game. Food was on the coffee tables, end tables, and everywhere in between. Leave it to Frank to make too much food. Brian later said they had to live off of Ramen, eggs, and beans for a while to make up for what she had spent between the grocery and shopping that weekend. The ice chest was full of beer and pop. I got up a few times to refill water for Megan and Suzanne. Me and Megan were sitting off to one side. Neither of us had any interest in the game. She was rubbing my aching back and shoulders and telling me about her day with the girls. Suzanne sat off to the other side on the floor between Keith's legs (he had brought in a chair from the kitchen). She didn't care about the game either and was doodling on some copy paper. Frank sat next to Brian on the loveseat. She was subtly icing his knee with a cold pop. She was mad, but she still loved him.

The brothers were loud and obnoxious. Serious stereotypes. Trevor's fiancée kept texting him and he was getting frustrated by the interruptions. Rob told him to silence his phone like he did. She'd get over it. I saw Frank shoot Brian a look that could have killed him on the spot. His eyes got wide and he put his hands up like a hostage and shook his head.

It was late when Brian's brothers FINALLY left. I was tired, sore, and over them. At the time, I thought he was the one GOOD apple out of the bunch. We cleaned up quickly and went to bed (well, the floor) and passed out cold until morning.

At breakfast, Frank was all tears about seeing us go. It was kind of funny, but also sad. When Keith was outside smoking and Megan was having a shower, Suzanne slipped the piece of copy paper she had been working on over to me. I flipped it over. It was a pencil sketch of me and Megan sitting together and looking into each other's eyes (minus the split lip). The detail was amazing!

"Thank you."

She smiled and got up to wash her plate.

Day at the park: By Suzanne

I needed a day. Just a day. And I got it. Campus was closed for Memorial Day in 2009! Keith had to work but he promised to take me out do dinner when he got home. A day to myself. It had been so long since I'd had one of those. I woke with the sun and immediately began caffeinating. I had toyed with different plans for the day but I settled on my long forgotten passion.

The weather was perfect. It was a light overcast and the breeze was shallow. I set up my easel on a hill overlooking the river. Woodland Mound Park was good for two things; walking your dog and looking into Kentucky. Everything was cast in a light blue hue from the overhanging clouds.

I had spent several hours the night before digging through closets in the house. My brushes were here, my canvases were there… I eventually scraped it all together. I stood in my spot for hours. I tuned out the barking dogs and the disc golf players. It was hard to convey the fresh air and smell of the landscape with a brush and paint. I had chosen to focus on a sparsely populated section of the river. I watched the boats go up and down the water and birds skimming the surface. At a little after noon, I stepped back from my easel. This was as good a stopping point for lunch as any.

"That's amazing!" The sudden but familiar voice behind me scared the shit out of me. I turned. Ian was smiling and looking over my work.

"Thanks. What are you doing here?"

"Campus holiday down here too. Decided I needed to put my nose in a book that I'm *not* going to be tested over."

"I'm stopping for a snack. Join me?"

"I think I can live with that."

We sat in the grass. I pulled a cloth cooler out of my book bag. I set the sandwich out and grapes on top. Ian pulled a squished granola bar out of his pocket.

I looked over at the paperback in his arms. "What book are you reading?"

Marie Joseph-Charles 77

He turned it so I could read the cover. I recognized the gold biohazard emblem on the cover immediately.

"It's got everything I could want; government conspiracies, cults with mind control drugs, bioterrorism, and robot spiders." He set the book in his lap.

"Have you gotten to the part where they figure out what the fleshy green bulbs are yet?"

"No! Wait! You've read it?"

"One of my favorites. A girl can't survive on the classics alone."

"That's awesome! Don't ruin it for me."

"Wouldn't dream of it. There was supposed to be a sequel but it never came out.'

"That's depressing."

"I know."

We sat in silence for a minute. "I didn't know you could do that." He pointed up at the easel. "The picture you did of me and Megan is amazing. It's hanging above my desk in my room. I didn't know you could paint too."

"I don't get to very often. At one point I was planning on using it to pay my way through school but, as Dad pointed out, they're called 'starving artists' for a reason."

"Just because you can't make a living off of it, that doesn't mean you shouldn't do it. That's really good."

I felt like I may have been blushing a little. "Thanks. Landscapes aren't my favorite thing to paint, but it got me out of the house and into the fresh air, so it was a win-win."

"What do you like to paint?"

"Whatever pops into my head. You know that picture in my hallway of the two silhouettes burning?"

"You did that?"

"Yeah. After me and Wes split. I was trying to feel like a phoenix rising from the flames but my heart, apparently, decided I was just burning."

"You did rise though."

"Kind of."

"Keith is a bit of a step up."

"Yeah. A bit."

We had finished our little picnic. "Do you mind if I pop a squat here and watch you while I read?"

I smiled. "Not at all!"

Help with Homework: By Suzanne

It just didn't feel right. I don't know how else to describe it. It just wasn't right. Keith and I were sitting together on the couch and watching a movie. I was between his legs and resting against his belly. It was something we'd done a hundred times, but it didn't feel right. It felt like eons since the last time we had spent time together so it should have been relaxing and enjoyable. It was anything but. It felt forced and unnatural.

About halfway through the movie, I felt a familiar rumbling. He had fallen asleep and started snoring. I got up and waked outside. It was dark, but the stars were bright. I lay in the grass in the front yard. I was barefoot and in my pajamas, but I didn't care. The June air was perfect. The bugs in the grass sang to me. I closed my eyes and tried to melt into the ground.

BZZZZZ. BZZZZZ. BZZZZ. My cell phone was buzzing in my pocket. I'd forgotten I had the damn thing with me.

I answered. "Hello?"

"Hey, Suz. Sorry to call so late." Ian sounded apologetic.

"No worries, Love. What's up?"

"I need help with this homework question."

"Okay. Shoot."

"Is form or function more important in the design of a building. Defend your answer."

"So, what's your question?"

"I don't get it."

"What's not to get? Is it more important that a building design *look* right for the client or have more *functionality?*"

"That's what I don't get. It has to have a balance of both."

"I don't think that's going to be a right answer. Do you think a client would be more happy with a building that looks great but hurts their productivity or one that meets their needs but looks like crap?"

"I don't know."

"Well, I think that's the point of the assignment."

"What is?"

"To make you question things."

"A client isn't going to let me build them a building they don't like."

"Right."

"But they won't want anything that hurts their bottom line, either."

"Right."

"Okay. If I were going to design a vet clinic for you. Would you like one that looks good on the outside and catches the public's eye or would you like one that streamlined your daily routine."

"I'm not answering that."

"Why not?"

I giggled. "You're cheating! If I answer and tell you why, you're going to submit it for your homework."

I heard laughing on the other end of the line. "But that's why I called you!"

"To cheat?"

More laughing. "Yeah!"

"Sorry, Love."

"Dammit. I'll call Frank."

"You wake her up and she'll kill you."

"Good point. I guess I'll try and answer it on my own."

"Yeah. Guess you'll have to."

"Good night."

"Good night, Love."

I turned off the phone and smiled. What a goober. I did love that he called me though. Not just that he had called me that night, but that he called in general. He picked up the phone and we heard each others' voices. I loved that. It meant so much more than a text message.

Work Picnic with Megan: by Ian

It felt like it was two hundred degrees out. It was August and the flies and mosquitoes were making a meal out of me. We had dug out tens of thousands of dollars worth of landscaping from this couple's property to lay out something different that still cost tens of thousands of dollars. I wish people understood how much it hurts to see people spend shit-tons of money just because they are bored. The house had to have had at least six bedrooms and as many bathrooms. There was a guest house, a four car detached garage (in addition to the garage that was attached to the house), and another building out by the badass in-ground pool. The couple wasn't that much older than me so I really wondered what they did for a living. The thing that really kicked me in the teeth was when I found out that they had all of this property and house but they lived alone! A house big enough to shelter half the homeless in Cincinnati and enough money to feed most of them regularly and it was all wasted. I had to kind of laugh when I saw my coworker unloading a statue of the Virgin Mary from the back of the truck. Wasn't there something about gluttony being a sin?

I hadn't seen Megan in about two weeks. Hell, I felt like I hadn't seen anyone but my mom in a month. It was summer and I was picking up extra shifts everywhere I could squeeze them in. Being broke sucks but luckily the landscaping company I worked for was family owned and they understood and helped me as much as they could

I was laying out trays of these ugly-as-Hell orange flowers when I heard her.

"That saffron color is really pretty there."

I smiled and turned to Megan. "I like your orange hair better."

"Not your best line."

"You caught me by surprise." I stood up and hugged her. "What are you doing here? Wait. How did you even find me?"

"You said you would be working in Indian Hill for the next few weeks so all I had to do was drive around aimlessly until I found the house with your company's trucks in the driveway."

I raised my eyebrow at her. "You didn't really do that, did you?"

"You really think I have nothing better to do? I called the main office and when I said who I was, the nice lady didn't have a problem giving me the address. Apparently, she's heard a lot about me." She smiled. I loved her smile.

"I may have mentioned you a time or two. That still doesn't tell me why you're here."   She stepped back and held up a picnic basket. "I'd love to have lunch with you but I've got a lot of work to do."

She pretended to pout. "Hey, Eddie!" She yelled over my shoulder.

My boss looked over at me. "Riker, go to lunch."

"You called my boss?!"

"Don't be silly. The nice lady in your main office did. I didn't want to come all the way out here for nothing!"

This woman was amazing. We sat under a tree and she unpacked the ultimate picnic. My favorite! Roast beef on rye with bacon, pickles, mustard, mayonnaise, and Swiss cheese, those little fake cheese saltine cracker things with the peanut butter in the middle, and chocolate chip cookies for desert. I was starving! I kissed her cheek and took a big bite out of the sandwich. She was still unwrapping her turkey club.

"I don't see how you can eat that." She looked pretty disgusted.

I washed down the sandwich with sport drink. "Yeah, well, I don't see how you can eat black olives so I guess we're even." While intentionally looking her in the eye I exaggerated another bite.

"Hardly."

While I stuffed my face, she told me about her plans to talk to city and the pyrotechnic experts that put on the fireworks display over the river every Labor Day. Something about wanting to know how the city has improved traffic flow for an event that draws thousands of people from surrounding states and how the pyrotechnics department can improve visibility so that people further away can enjoy the show. I don't really know exactly what her point was in all of it. That sandwich was amazing.

Marie Joseph-Charles 83

At one point, I glanced up and noticed that my coworkers were attempting to not make it obvious that they were pissed that I was enjoying lunch with a beautiful redhead while they were still working so I told Megan I had to go back to work. She looked sad.

"Okay." She kissed my cheek. "Can we try to see each other again sometime before another two weeks are up?"

That made me really sad and feel kind of selfish. I hugged her. "I'm sorry I've been busy."

"I know you are but I miss you."

"I miss you, too." I kissed her. "I'll text you when I get done here."

"Okay, Architect." She squeezed my hand and left.

I am a horrible, horrible boyfriend. I worked until after dark and Eddie made me go home. I was exhausted and dehydrated. Mom was already asleep when I got home. I got a shower and was going to fix myself something hearty to eat but passed out cold at the kitchen table with a bowl of cereal instead. I never texted her.

I tried over and over again to get a hold of her on my way to work the next morning. I thought she was pissed but she wasn't. She told me later that she was just sad but she understood. I felt like such a dick.

When I got to the jobsite. I looked at the orange flowers and I got an idea.

I messaged Suzanne. *"Can I commission a painting?"*
"Of what?"

I sent her a few pictures of the flowers.

She messaged back. *"LOL. Most men just get the girl the flowers, not commission a painting. You must have really messed up. I'll have it done ASAP"*.

A week later a courier presented Megan with an eight by ten painted canvas of those awful orange flowers she liked so much. The note read: *Most men just get the girl flowers, not commission a painting. I really messed up.* Thanks for the message, Suz!

The Proposal: by Suzanne

January 21st, 2010 was my dad's sixty-seventh birthday. He was old compared to most people my age's parents. I was a "happy oops" (as Daddy put it) that occurred late in life for him. He'd married a woman half his age after only knowing her a few months because she was energetic and made him feel young. Talking to my aunts and uncles, he was a sugar daddy that went too far. I don't know how true that is. I don't have a relationship with my mom, so I can't ask her. Despite everything that she had put him through and the fact that I looked *exactly* like her, he still treated me like I was his most valuable possession.

We were having dinner at a cheesy Chinese restaurant/buffet. I offered to take him somewhere nice or, at least, where most of the menu items were recognizable. He insisted that he loved the fried rice there and that's what he wanted for his big day. I think he was just trying to spare my wallet.

"Tell me about life!" We had barely sat in the rickety booth and tucked in our coats.

"What is there to tell? School is brutal. I'm awake for days at a time and the other day I was driving and hallucinated a vulture flying into my windshield and almost wrecked my car."

"That's not good. You need to take better care of yourself. You'll put yourself into an early grave."

"Dead people don't have to pay back student loans."

"That's not funny. How is Keith?"

"He's Keith. He's been working from home a lot more after hours and he's mad because it's taking time away from the car."

"Does he take care of you?"

"As much as he can. I'm hardly home. Two days ago I fell asleep in one of the stalls in the large animal ICU. Thank God the kid who found me said it happens all the time and didn't tell anyone. When I am home, he makes sure I remember to eat and tries to make sure I get some sleep in where I can."

"I repeat, you are going to put yourself into an early grave."

"You shouldn't have instilled so much drive in me."

"Touché."

Marie Joseph-Charles 85

"Besides. I have two more years and I'm home free!"

The waitress arrived to take our order. She appeared so suddenly and quietly that she startled me completely. She was petite and didn't speak English very well but she was exceptionally polite.

After our order was placed, my dad turned to me. "You know what I want for my birthday next year?"

I did NOT like where this was going. "What?"

"To walk my little Button down the isle."

I rolled my eyes and exhaled loudly. "Dad. Don't call me that."

"You remember why I call you that, right?"

I took a deep breath again. "Because when I was little and mom was having one of her episodes, you told me that my smile was what held our family together. And I touched your shirt and said 'like a button.'"

"Exactly. I don't know how long I'm going to be around and I want to know that your smile is going to be buttoning together a family that you've started."

"Do you have any idea how much you sound like a '80s sitcom dad?"

"I may have rehearsed that a little."

"Are you dying?"

"Sweetheart. I'm sixty-seven years old. I could have a coronary next Tuesday."

"Dad. I don't want to get married."

"A birthday present isn't about what you want. It's about what I want."

"I think I have a voice in this one."

"Why are you so against marriage?"

"It's just so… final. 'Til death do you part.' You are forever bound legally and in the eyes of God until the sweet release of death."

"You make it sound like a prison sentence." He crossed his arms.

"Isn't it? Can you imagine my life if I had married Wes? I've made bad decisions about men before."

"How long have you and Keith been together now?"

"Almost four years."

"Don't you love him?"

"Of course I do. That doesn't mean he's the one I'm supposed to be with until I die."

"And if he's not, divorce is an option."

"Then why did you opt to be the good Catholic and stay married to Angela?"

"I wish you wouldn't insist on calling her by her first name. She is your mother."

"A mother is more than just someone who gave you fifty percent of your DNA.:

He ignored me. "I said it was an option for *you.* Not me."

"A lengthy, expensive, emotionally devastating process. Great option. Or… I can stay unmarried and if it isn't meant to be, we just break up clean and clear and I send him packing out of my house."

"Button. You have an awfully bleak outlook on life."

"Can you blame me?"

"But if you get married, there are insurance benefits and tax deductions. I know you need those. I know how much you've got in student loans that will start coming due before you know it and I know how much a starting veterinarian makes."

Okay. He had *one* good point. I was not at all happy with this conversation. I looked in his eyes. "You know she can't be there."

The 'she' I referred to was my mother. I guess I'd better explain my hatred for the woman who had given me life. After I was born, she 'just wasn't the same' according to my dad. Back then, they really didn't have a good grasp on post partum depression. Or any real mental health issues, for that matter. My only memories of her involve her being angry a lot and generally bat shit crazy. When I was about two, I had a baby brother born. He supposedly died of SIDS but given my mom's behavior (what I remember of it) from when I was young, she likely killed him.

As I got older, she became progressively more erratic. She would go on binges where she would drink herself into a stupor every day for a few weeks to a few months. That was when she was home. Sometimes she would get in the car and drive away and we stopped wondering if or when she would come back. Her re-emergences would usually coincide with when she would run out of money. When she would disappear, Daddy would move most of the money into a new account, leaving enough in the old account that he was sure she would be able to eat for a little while. She refused to take her meds most of the time (when we could get her help) and when she would take them, they were often chased with alcohol.

It all came to a head when I was thirteen. She pulled a knife on me for dressing like a whore (I was wearing a two-piece bathing suit and shorts) in front of my friends. My dad had to tackle her and wrestle it away. Some of my friends stopped talking to me after that. The ones that remained just pitied me. Dad talked to Aunt Dorinda and they had her committed to Good Sam psyche ward. She's been there ever since. I haven't seen her since the day they pulled her off of Daddy at the Hospital. She had started by crying and saying she would change. When he refused to cave, she lunged passed Aunt Dori and attacked him. Borderline personality disorder with bipolar disorder was her official diagnosis (in case you were wondering where my anxiety and depression stemmed from). Don't tell me mental health isn't genetic. Thanks for the awesome gift, Mom.

"I know, Button. I wouldn't expect her to be there in any way other than spirit."

"Will an exorcist keep that out?"

"Now, now." He smiled.

"What if I want to finish school and have a career first?"

"You're already living in sin. What's a little ceremony and cake?"

"You say that as if this will be a completely painless surgical procedure."

"Does this mean you will consider it?"

"*Consider*. That's it."

I haven't seen him smile that big in years.

That night, when I went home to Keith, my wedding proposal was more like a business proposition. I explained what my dad had said and that he really wanted this and that, as much as I hated to admit it, I could really use his benefits.

Marie Joseph-Charles 88

Keith looked bright. "Let's do it!"

"Really?" I was kind of hoping he would be the foot in the ground on this one. "Just like that?"

"Do you have any idea how long I've wanted to call you my wife?" He kissed my forehead.

I suddenly felt the urge to run and vomit.

My Future In-Laws: By Suzanne

Keith's parents had insisted on holding an engagement celebration dinner. As if this was something to celebrate. I really didn't want to go but since it was kind of in my honor, I didn't really have a choice. Rhonda, Keith's mom, had insisted and Lord knows I couldn't say 'no' to his mother. I wouldn't call him a mama's boy, but he was pretty close.

Of course, they insisted that I take a Saturday night off of work for this debacle. It's not like I was a full-time college student and needed money or anything. The frosting on this festivity was when they chose a large chain buffet restaurant that was well known in the area to cause food poisoning. I had enough trouble choking the food down the few times I had gone before. It was spongy and lukewarm and gross. Who decided an unattended chocolate fountain was a good idea? Who let that kid put a chicken nugget in it?

Suck it up, Suzanne. Let's do this.

We were seated at a table of questionable cleanliness. Rhonda was a nice woman but not necessarily the brightest. She was a hairdresser at one of those cheap walk-in places and I think she'd huffed a little too much hairspray. She was always trying to keep up with the latest trends and her nails were always long and fake and I wondered how she kept from stabbing her customers with them. When we first met, she kept touching my hair and telling me about all of the wonderful things she could do with hair like mine. I told her, as politely as I could, there was no way she would ever be allowed to cut my hair. I was initially afraid I had hurt her feelings but Keith told me not to feel bad about it. He said Frank had told her the same thing repeatedly when they were growing up.

Rhonda's second husband was Dan. She'd cheated on Keith's dad with him and they were married shortly after the divorce. Keith didn't think highly of him at all and blamed him a lot for breaking up his family. I wanted to remind him that Rhonda wasn't exactly innocent in the whole thing but it didn't take me long to realize it was just better if I kept my mouth shut. Dan wasn't someone I particularly cared for. He chain smoked, just

like the rest of them and was know to drink pretty heavily. He was
the "man's man" from an all-boys club and I couldn't stand it.

We went through the buffet line. Most of the food was
barely recognizable. I carefully selected a few items to be polite.
I'd eat a real dinner when I got home. We returned to the table and
I pushed some still-frozen broccoli under a blob that I as pretty
sure was mashed potatoes. Rhonda didn't notice. She was
excitedly prattling on over how she was so excited for us and that
she could do the wedding party's hair. Over my dead body.

She and Keith finished their plates and went back for
seconds. How they could stomach this stuff was beyond me.

Dan and I sat in silence for a few minutes before he looked
at me from across the table. "You still in school?"

"Yup. Two years to go."

"Really? You going to go through with it?"

I was kind of startled by the question. "Why wouldn't I?"

Keith sat down next to me. "They brought out fresh steak!"

I don't know what was on his plate, but that didn't look like
beef.

Dan spoke up. "Well, you're going to be a wife now."

I coked my head at him. "And?"

"Well, I just don't see how you plan on balancin' a home
and school."

"Um. Same way I have been."

"It's overwhenling ain't it?"

"Yeah. But I'm managing."

"Maybe you should just make things a little easier on
yourself and your future husband."

I looked at Keith. He was happily stuffing his face and
seemed oblivious to the conversation.

I looked Dan dead in the eye. "What *exactly* are you trying
to say?"

"You should probably give up now, before you get in too
deep."

"*What?!*" I couldn't believe what he was saying.

"It's just... You're going to fail. I know you are."

"So just because *you* think I'm wasting my time, I should just throw away the last six years of blood and sweat?" I was seething.

"It'll probably be better. Then you can be at home more."

I was fighting back tears. I looked at Keith. He looked at me and shrugged his shoulders, his mouth full of food. That was it. A shrug. He didn't try to defend me. He didn't even attempt to deescalate the situation.

I stood up just as Rhonda returned to the table. I looked at her. "Thank you for dinner." I turned to Keith. "You can ride home with them."

It was a forty minute drive home. I choked back the tears and focused on the anger. How dare he? How dare *they*? Dan 'knows I'm going to fail' and Keith may as well have backed him up. She sure as Hell didn't back *me* up. I turned it over and over in my mind. What if he was right? What if I did fail? No. I've worked to hard and come too far. How could Keith not support me? How was this marriage supposed to work?

When I got home, I curled up in bed with Ariel. He tried to use his healing purr to bring me down. It slowly worked.

My phone beeped. I was sure it was Keith asking if I'd come back for him. No. It was Rhonda. *"I'm so sorry about what Dan said. You know how he can get."*

Yeah. I didn't respond.

It was about another hour or so before Keith made his way home. I was already changed into my pajamas and in bed.

He came in the bedroom and turned on the light. "You didn't have to leave like that."

I sat up and looked at him. "I don't need to be around people who think I'm going to fail."

"It's Dan. He's just talking out his ass."

"It doesn't matter. I don't want to be around that.."

"You didn't have to leave me there."

"You seemed to be enjoying your steak."

He rolled his eyes. "Whatever. Mom feels really bad about it."

"Why? She didn't do anything wrong." Except pick an absolutely disgusting restaurant that I hated.

"She yelled at Dan for being insensitive."

Awesome. At least my future mother-in-law will stand up for me.

"Okay. I'll thank her tomorrow."

He stood silent for a moment. "I'm going to stay up for a bit."

"Fine." I rolled back over.

He shut the door.

I lay there in the dark, awake, for hours. I felt so completely alone.

Christmas to remember by Ian

It's kind of funny how something little can make a day really memorable. We had barely seen each other in two years. Frank and Suzanne were away for school. I had school, work, and mom. Keith worked overtime a lot and Megan had her own school and work life. We sent each other text messages and talked on the phone when we could. I would send Suz pictures of places I went hiking to cheer her up since she couldn't go.

But the holidays were a special mess. There was traveling and multiple families' houses to go to. So, for whatever reason, Keith and Suzanne decided to have a Christmas dinner at their house for all of us. I have no doubt it wasn't Suzanne's idea. I know she missed us but I would more likely see her ordering pizza for us all. She would never intentionally put herself under that much strain. My gut was telling me it had more to do with Keith and Brian's incognito macho rivalry and Suz's sanity was collateral damage.

It was cold and wet but not snowy. Just a typical, miserable Cincinnati winter night. It was a few days before Christmas. We had all agreed that December twenty fourth and twenty fifth were not options since we all had multiple families to visit. Megan, Brian, and Frank were the only ones who had parents who were still together. Since Brain's parents lived further west and he had a Christmas with them and one with his brothers and Frank had Christmas with her parents separate from her grandparents, they had four family Christmases spread over 400 miles, Christmas together, and now this. I kind of pitied them.

Inside Suzanne's home, though, it was warm. She had been trying her best to bake in her little kitchen. She made a roast goose, which I thought was pretty impressive. She said she didn't trust her skills to get a turkey right and she was sure we would all get trichinosis (whatever that is) if she tried to make a ham but she knew she could do a goose right. I think her parasitology course was getting to her a little. When Megan and I arrived, Brian and Keith were in the garage talking loudly about the car. Suzanne was fussing over a few pots on the stove and Frank was trying to make sure the table was set just right.

Marie Joseph-Charles 94

I had my arms full of presents and I could barely see where I was going when Ariel decided it was a good time to run between my legs. I would have lost it completely if Megan hadn't somehow caught the boxes I was dropping while steadying me at the same time.

Frank looked up and smiled. "Hey! Here! Don't you dare put those just anywhere under the tree! It has to look perfect!" She rushed over to me and took the boxes from me one by one and arranged them the way she wanted. "They're wrapped so pretty! Megan must have done it."

Megan snickered at me and went into the kitchen. I guess Suzanne was a frazzled mess. Unlike Frank, she was not a prissy entertainer with too many magazine subscriptions. She was just going to be happy if it turned out edible. She was wearing a red plaid shirt over a white turtle neck. There was food and white powder all over her nice black jeans and her hair looked a little like she had stuck her finger in a light socket.

Megan looked around the kitchen and then to Suzanne. "Wine?"

Suzanne laughed. "Oh my God, that sounds wonderful."

Frank grabbed my arm "Two more. And make it the Vidal Blanc."

Dinner really was good. I had never had a roasted goose before and I really liked it. We had all brought something of our own family traditions (at Frank's request) to add to the meal. In addition to the goose, Suzanne made homemade bread. Megan had made green bean casserole that wasn't too bad. I don't think the topping was supposed to be soggy. Brian had made some kind of baked sweet potato thing with marshmallows on top. He said he new it was gross but he was told he had to bring a family tradition and that was something that his family had at every meal. None of us touched it. Frank made pies for desert, of course. I had made spinach dumplings. I have no idea how that tradition got started, but my Aunt Leena always brought them for dinners at our house. Keith made canned corn. I always knew his mom couldn't cook, but I didn't know it was that bad!

After dinner, we were all in the living room digesting. Frank and Brian were stretched out on the couch together. Megan and I had squeezed together in Keith's recliner and Keith was in Suzanne's rocking chair. I kind of felt bad about Suzanne sitting on the floor, but she had picked that spot before any of us sat down and she seemed happy with her ginger tea and her cat on her lap.

"Okay! What was everyone's favorite Christmas gift they got when they were a kid?" Frank couldn't just let us sit in peace.

Brian piped up. "Easy. My black monster truck Power Wheel."

Keith piped up. "Oh yeah! Twelve volts of power was awesome when you were a kid!"

"Now nothing less than one seventy five HP will do!"

"Go big or go home!" They high-fived each other and Frank almost got dumped on the floor in the process.

"Sorry, Babe. What was yours?" Brian tried to smooth over the situation a little.

"My mom got me one of those little kid's nurse's kits with the fake stethoscope that actually worked. She thought I would want to be a nurse. Nope. My half-siblings don't want to have anything to do with me so I played with the animals in the neighborhood. Poof! Here I am! Going to be a veterinarian in a few short years!"

"A kick-ass veterinarian." Brian kissed the top of her. He obviously wanted to make sure she wasn't mad about almost hitting the floor.

Megan spoke up. "Mine's kind of the opposite. My dad was mad that I was a girl and tried to treat me like one. Everything I owned was pink and I had an ungodly number of baby dolls. He doesn't believe a woman can do what a man can do. One year he got me a baby doll that would wet its diaper after you gave it a bottle. He said I needed to prepare for being a wife and mother while I was still young. I was nine. I was old enough to know he was belittling me so I have spent over ten years since then proving to him that I am more than a house wife. So I guess it wasn't my favorite gift, but definitely the most influential." She looked at me. "What about you?"

I looked at the Christmas tree. I could see all of us reflected back in one of the shiny silver balls. The reflection was curved, of course, but we really looked like a family; not just a group of (mostly) college kids trying our hand at adulting.

"Well?" Frank was so pushy.

"I guess it was probably a GI Joe that my sister gave me. I was four. It was the last Christmas before my dad left. Karen had been saving her allowance and bought it for me with her own money. After Dad left and she hated me, I used to get it out and pretend that we were still a family and relive that day over and over."

"That's really sweet." Frank was forever the optimist.

"Yeah, well, when I was seven Karen got pissed and broke it in half to get back at me for supposedly ruining her slumber party."

"Well that's depressing. Why don't we open some presents and liven things up a little?" Leave it to Keith to want to change the subject.

"Yes. Honey, why don't you hand them out?" Frank sat up so Brian could go to the tree.

"But I'm comfortable." Idiot move. Frank gave him *that look* and he immediately got up and sat on the floor by the tree.

Suzanne had been sitting next to the tree in silence all along. She seemed happy to just sip her tea and pet her cat and listen to us.

Brian picked up the first present. "To Frank from Megan."

"Gimme!" Frank tore through that paper like a dog with a new toy. "New scrubs! YES! Thank you!"

Okay, to save time I'll explain that we were pretty much all barely surviving college kids so Megan and I had both gotten Suz and Frank different sets of scrubs for school. We chipped in together and got Keith some special wrench he had said he was going to need soon and I think we got Brian football tickets.

"To Ian from Suzanne."

He handed me something square and about the size of a small board game box but it was heavy. I opened it. It was a faux leather-bound blank book. The front was embossed 'Ian Riker Original Designs.' I looked at Suzanne.

She smiled. "I know you hate using the computer programs for your designs. I thought you might like something to keep your hand-drawn ones all together. It may be worth something someday. Like Robling designs or something."

That was it. The most thoughtful thing anyone had gotten me in a very long time. It wasn't something I had asked for or even knew I needed. She just knew *me*. I suddenly had a new favorite Christmas present.

Marie Joseph-Charles 98

Christmas 2010: by Suzanne

I really wasn't happy with Keith. I wasn't sure how he had conned me into putting on a fancy dinner for six people. He kept reminding me it was a small group of familiar faces, so I wouldn't need to go all out. He said it would be great practice for when our parents were old and we had to have family meals at our house. Fat chance. Under no foreseeable circumstance was his stepdad to place a single toe in my house and there was even less of a chance that I would cook for him unless it had a little arsenic seasoning. Better yet, cyanide supposedly tastes like almonds. I could bake a cherry pie with an almond crumb topping… What? Everyone hates at least one of their in-laws.

We settled on Monday the twentieth. Keith was pouting. His brilliant idea had backfired in that we would be eating while the Bears vs Vikings would be on. Karma. I spent two weeks creating a menu. Everyone kept telling me they would all bring a dish to contribute and then Frank came up with some brilliant idea to make it a "family tradition dish." Why? Because she's Frank and we love her so we all went along.

I could go easy on myself and do chicken. No. My chicken always came out "drier than a worm in the desert," as Keith frequently told me. Classic ham dinner? No. I could cook it wrong and kill us all. Whole turkey? Absolutely not. Not after the masterpiece that Frank created at Thanksgiving two years prior. I could cook a pretty damn good roasted goose. Strange talent, I know. Okay. We have a main dish. Now we just need appetizers, maybe a soup course, salads, wine (of course), and sides. And it all has to go together. Maybe we should just do BLTs and chips.

December twentieth at five was show time. I got a 9 pound goose. He was little, but money was a bit tight since this wasn't something I had been able to properly prepare for. Okay. Goose would take three hours and forty five minutes to cook. Maybe four hours if I open the oven too often. So that didn't need to go into the oven until 1pm. I needed to start making h'orderves early so I wouldn't be scrambling to get them done as the guests arrive. Strawberry Santa hats with marshmallow pompoms. Gingerbread reindeer heads with pretzel antlers and red gumdrop noses. Cheese tray with cheese, crackers, and fruit arranged to look like a wreath. Braided bread. Better get that started early too in case I screw it up and need to make another one. Maybe I should do dinner rolls too, just in case. Don't forget the salad! Keith could throw on his corn in the final five.

I had everything going at once. The oven was full of cookies and a piddly little goose. All four burners on the stove were spoken for. I was even cooking the bread in the toaster oven. My strawberry Santa hats were in a storage container on the back porch to stay cold because the fridge was full of wine, a giant salad bowl, a cheese tray wreath, and more wine.

Frank and Brian arrived a little after four. They brought pies (that were put out with the strawberries), a casserole dish that I was instructed to put in the oven in the last thirty minutes, and hey! More wine!

Frank insisted on helping set up the table. "You look like you've been at this all day!"

"What's your point?"

Brian and Keith took a few beers and headed out to the garage as always.

At just before five, Ian and Megan came in. Frank hurried to head them off and I was glad for a few seconds in the kitchen alone. It must have been a category four that blew through my kitchen that day. There was flour and cornstarch all over the counters, the floor, and me. We had run out of space in the dishwasher and were washing dishes and piling them on the counter as we went. Keith had come in and stolen a chunk of my cheese tray after Frank had set it out. It was definitely not the magazine cover that Frank had created for Thanksgiving. It was embarrassing to say the least.

No one seemed to care about the state of the kitchen. That was a huge relief to me. Frank and Ian complemented my goose and Megan polished off like five rolls. All in all, dinner seemed to be a success and it really was nice to have us all in the same room, around the same table again.

After dinner, I put the kettle on and made tea for me and Megan. We piled into the living room. I strategically sat next to the tree to block Keith's view of the tiny box he hadn't noticed yet. In five days, I would wake up early and make coffee, bacon, eggs, and biscuits. We would have a nice Christmas breakfast and then sit next to the tree. He would open the little box and find the gear shift knob that I had been squirreling away money for months to buy him.

I sat and listened to everyone's stories of their favorite gifts. I secretly hoped they wouldn't ask me. I had a thirty year old teddy bear that my grandpa Joe and grandma Ellen had gotten me but, other than that, I really didn't have a favorite gift. I felt kind of pathetic about that. I was relieved when they decided to open presents instead. It was kind of amusing how Frank could control Brian with just a look. It was clear who wore the pants in that relationship.

I have to say, I was seriously excited by the scrubs from Ian and Megan. They weren't the cheap ten-dollar-a-set unisex ones I usually bought myself with my work stipend. These were at last twenty five dollars and fit me right.

When I saw Ian open his present, I suddenly felt nervous. What if he didn't like it? I had thought so hard about what to get him. He wasn't a car or sports guy like Brian and Keith. I also had this unexplainable need to do something a little more special for him than I did for the others. I was relieved when he smiled after I explained it and he kept rubbing his hand over it in his lap, so I assumed that was a good thing. I just hoped he didn't rub the lettering off.

"There's one more. Looks like it's for Frank." Brian held up a decorative hat box that I hadn't noticed before.

"But I already got a present from everyone." She reached out and took the box from him.

"Maybe it's a secret Santa thing," Megan offered.

Frank lifted the lid and folded back some tissue paper. Her eyes bulged and her head shot up. She looked at Brian who was kneeling on the floor. "Are you fucking serious?!"

"Woah!" Ian exclaimed. Frank didn't swear nearly as much as the rest of us.

"As a heart attack." Brian took the box from her and held the ring out.

Marie Joseph-Charles 101

"Not the most romantic answer, but I'll take it!" She looked like she was going to cry.

"Is that a 'yes'?" He slid the ring on her left hand.

"Oh my God! Yes!" She launched herself off of the couch and into his arms, knocking him backwards into the tree.

We were all laughing. I looked at Megan and Ian. Megan wiggled her eyebrows at him. He shook his head. I laughed harder.

Bridal Dress Shopping by Suzanne

So Frank decided that we needed to help her do some pre-dress-shopping shopping. She wanted Cathy's input on the final dress, of course, but she wanted her best friends there to help her narrow down the choices first. I think it was because there would be a bit less pressure with us. Her mom had wanted this for her since Frank was in diapers and would likely go into hock making it her perfect day rather than Frank's.

Frank made a brunch-time appointment for us at one of those fancy bridal boutiques in February of 2011. I was late, as usual, and rushed in in time to see Frank and Megan being ushered towards a back room. I hurried up to them.

"Ah, excellent! The maid of honor?" The sequined and heavily makeup-ed older woman who was escorting them smiled at me with a creepy, toothy, fake smile.

Frank took my arm. "No. My best friend. But she is in the bridal party."

"I see." The sparkly clown lady turned her back towards me.

Megan giggled behind her hand and pointed. The lady wore large, pointed red shoes like a witch or clown but that wasn't what made her giggle. The back of the lady's black skirt was partially unzipped and gave a rather unflattering view of a red lace thong. Not what one would expect in a seventy-ish year old woman. I maintained my composure but on the inside I was dying of laughter.

We were taken up an elevator to a large room. The wall directly in front of us was made of ceiling height windows and overlooked the city. The wall to the right contained five curtained fitting rooms. The wall we had walked through and to the left were all mirrors. In the center was a faux leather platform that looked kind of like an overpriced ottoman. A large group of chairs was arranged in a semi-circle around the ottoman and every second chair was spaced out with a small, dark table. A long, matching table was in front of the windows. I wondered what that was for.

Megan leaned into me (we were behind Sparkles the Clown and Frank). "Holy shit!"

Marie Joseph-Charles 103

I leaned back to her. "I know!"

"Will there be others?" Sparkles looked to Frank.

"No. Not today. The appointment I have scheduled in six weeks will be for the rest of the bridal party.

"Very well. I will send Lisa in to see to you in a moment." She backed out the door and closed it.

Megan and I lost it. We fell into two of the chairs laughing. Frank looked completely confused so we explained Sparkles's wardrobe malfunction. Frank laughed too.

Suddenly, the door burst open and a peppy brunette in a long skirt and ruffled blouse came in. She had a binder and a grocery scanner in her left hand. She rushed over to Frank and shook her hand. "Hi! I'm Lisa! I'll be your personal assistant throughout the process of making your wedding dreams come true!"

Megan and I stood up and looked at each other. It was as if we both knew this day was going to be much more than we bargained for.

Lisa continued. "Bridesmaids gowns are directly below us on floor five. Bridal gowns are the two floors below that. Traditional gowns are on the fourth floor and nontraditional are on floor three." What did she mean by 'nontraditional' gowns? "When the groom and groomsmen come, tuxedos can be found on floor two. Here is your scanner. Take a bit, stroll through and scan anything you think you might like." She pressed the scanner into Frank's hand. "Don't worry. This is a process so if you don't scan it, that doesn't mean it's off the table. When you are ready, come back here and hit the buzzer by the door and it'll alert me that you're ready. I'll download the information from the scanner and we'll get started! I've got the measurements you sent me right here." She placed her hand on the binder. "There will need to be some adjusting on a lot of these so keep that in mind. While you're gone, we'll finish setting up here!"

"Oh. Okay. Back to the elevator we came up?" Frank looked at the scanner in her hand.

"Yes! Or the stairs are at the opposite end of the hall if you prefer."

"Okay. Thank you."

"You're very welcome! We'll see you soon!"

We exited the door. We looked towards the elevator and saw a group of men in chef's hats pushing carts of food towards us.

"Guess we're taking the stairs. I wonder who that's for." Megan had her wide-eyed look back on.

We turned away from the food carts and headed down the stairs.

"Let's stop at the bridesmaids gowns and breeze through really quick. I still don't know exactly what I'm looking for for you guys. Megan, are you sure I can't convince you to be in my wedding?" Frank looked pouty as we wondered through rows of mannequins, gowns on hangers, and mirrors. It was all very overwhelming, if I'm going to be honest.

"I'll be *at* your wedding. As much as I think of you as more than a friend, I just don't feel quite like I'm at that 'bridesmaid' place."

"Okay. That's fair. I am glad you're here." Frank smiled and took Megan's arm.

"Me too." Megan smiled back.

'Oh, I like this!" Frank dropped Megan's arm and ran to the most God-awful cotton candy pink taffeta dress ever created. She lifted the scanner to the barcode on the hanger.

My brain: *Oh HELL no! There is no way I am even thinking about putting that on.* My mouth: "Drop the scanner." Frank looked at me. I had to think fast. "We aren't here for our dresses. Today is about your dress!"

"I suppose you're right." Frank backed away from the dress and led the charge back to the stairwell.

Megan giggled. "Nice save."

I grinned. "I don't know what you're talking about."

"Yeah, right. You would be so pretty in pink." She nudged me with her elbow.

"Keep it up. If I have to wear that thing, so do you; even if I have to poison one of her cousins to make it happen."

Megan laughed loudly. Frank looked disappointed that she wasn't in on the joke as we exited on the 'traditional gown' floor. Megan thought quickly. "We were just saying how the men get lost trying to shop in a department store. They're doomed when we set them loose here."

"Oh, I've already thought of that. Their assistant for the day is not to leave them unsupervised. It's not that I don't trust Brian. Let's face it. It's his brothers that will be the problem." She turned back to the gowns.

I leaned over to Megan. "Nice save."

She giggled.

I didn't know there could possibly be that many types of gowns to choose from. Most of the ones on the traditional floor were white and floor length (or longer). Most had long sleeves, lace, v-necks... They were all very elegant and classy. The nontraditional floor was a bit more fun. There were different colors ranging from cream or silver to holy-shit-blue. Many of the white ones had brightly colored lace accents, bows, or embroidery. A lot of them were fairly short and/or sleeveless or had the option to be sleeveless. Then, there was the wall of heads. It had to have been close to a hundred fake heads with tiaras, veils, and various combinations of the two. I was so glad this was all for her, not me. There was no way I would have survived an anxiety attack of the magnitude I would have had had I been in Frank's shoes. I didn't have to shop for a dress at all and my wedding planning panic hadn't kicked in yet.

After what felt like eternity (it turned out to actually only be like forty minutes), Frank was satisfied with her amount of scanning and we returned to our room. Turned out, those carts of food were for us. The table in front of the windows was now heavily decked out in silver tableware, fruit, muffins, orange juice, an ice bucket with champagne, and more.

Frank pressed the buzzer for Lisa. I flopped in a chair. Megan started pouring glasses of champagne.

"Cathy is going to enjoy this a little too much, I think." I took a glass from Megan as Frank sat on the ottoman/stage thing.

"Tell me about it. We'd be down there scanning dresses 'til next Tuesday if she had come along today!" Frank laughed.

"You're lucky she wants to be such a big part of your life." Megan sipped her champagne.

"Sometimes. Sometimes I think she just wants to live through me."

"I think most moms do to some extent." Megan took another sip.

I laughed. "Not mine."

"She would if she could. Do you think they'll ever let her out?" Frank was wringing her hands a little. I think she was afraid to ask the question.

"Sure. If she stays on her meds for more than a few months straight. She doesn't want to 'poison' herself with drugs."

"Are they sure she's not schizophrenic?" Megan looked me in the eye.

"It's been tossed around. It wouldn't surprise me. I honestly don't know what *all* is wrong with her. All I know is if she really wanted to be part of my life, she would stick to treatment. I know it's not all in her control because she's sick but I do know she used to be pretty lucid and at least putting forward *some* effort would show me *something*."

"I guess that makes sense." Megan finished her champagne and went for more. This time, she picked up the whole bucket and set it on the little end table between us.

"At least your mom isn't part of your life because she's sick. My brother and sister are just assholes." Frank held out her glass for a refill.

"They really aren't coming to your wedding?" Megan poured us all a round.

"Nope. The only reason I went to Lorenzo's wedding is because I was too young to have a say in the matter and Dad made me. When Sophia got married, I refused to go. They made it perfectly clear when I was growing up and they would be at my house on the weekends that we are NOT family."

"I don't get it. It's not like it's your fault their mom and your dad split." Megan was shaking her head.

"I know. And it was their mom who left and filed for divorce. Not to mention, Mom and Dad didn't get married until years later. He had moved on with his life and I guess I'm a reminder of that."

Just then, the door burst open and in comes Lisa followed by a rack holding a couple dozen wedding dresses. "Are we ready?!"

Cue the eighties music montage. The first dress was SO POOFY! It was all hands on deck to get her in it. When I asked what she was going to do if she had to pee, she nixed that dress and another two that were just as poofy. The next one made her look like a frosted cupcake. The next one couldn't contain her boobs. I'm not sure how much help Megan and I were being. We were getting champagne drunk and sugar high off of the chocolate muffins. I remember a lot of giggling.

At one point, Frank was spinning on the ottoman/stage while looking in the mirror. The dress wasn't bad. It was long and flowing but sleeveless with embroidered bright red rose stencils starting at the bodice and cascading down the front of the dress. It wasn't my style, but I liked it. Frank couldn't decide.

"If you get that one, you won't need a bouquet! It's already on the dress! Though tossing it to all the single women might be a bit of a problem!" Megan fell over laughing. She was pretty drunk.

Frank laughed. "Keep it up. I'll give you shit when it's your turn, too." She stepped down off the ottoman and went to the rack to select the next dress.

"One step at a time! Let's get a man to say 'I love you' first and take it from there."

I almost choked on the orange slice I was eating. Frank spun around hard and almost lost her balance from the weight of the dress. "Ian *still* hasn't told you he loves you?!"

Megan's eyes got wide again and she sat upright as if she was suddenly sober. "Well. No."

"What the Hell is he waiting for?" Frank held her arms out and the seamstress began unpinning the dress.

"I don't know. I just assumed he knows how serious those words are and wants to wait until the right time."

"I get it but it's been like four years."

"I'm not going to rush him. Life's been kind of hard between work, school, his mom, and all that."

"But still! Four years!" Frank was zipped into a new gown and stood on the ottoman again.

"They're just words. What matters is that he acts like it. I'd rather a guy never say it but show me every day than tell me every day but act like I'm just there for the sake of being there." I tried to defend poor Megan.

"Something you want to talk about?" Frank looked straight at me as her dress was pinned.

"Let's just say I envy you two sometimes."

"Do I need to kick some ass? We're family so I can!" Frank put her hands on her hips.

Megan and I laughed at her feeble attempt to look stern while being pinned in a sparkly… I don't even know what to call that "dress."

Frank sighed and stopped the seamstress from pinning the rest. She could tell by our faces that it was a definite 'no." I was glad to have the attention moved away from me.

Wedding Prep for Men: By Ian

I'm not sure which surprised me more; that Suzanne and Keith were actually getting married or that he asked me to be his best man. Don't get me wrong, I was honored. We had been family forever but he had a step brother to consider. As for them actually getting married—let's just say I was waiting for Suz to run screaming into the night right up until I saw her walk down the isle. She had been vehemently against marriage as long as I knew her. I knew this wasn't her idea. I also knew getting married while she was still in school wasn't her idea. She had tried to dig her heels in to wait until after she graduated but her dad was pressuring her to have it sooner. He kept saying he wanted to make sure he was alive to see it. To be honest, I thought it was pretty manipulative and disgusting on his part. It was obvious the reason he wanted it as soon as possible is because he didn't want her to have a chance to change her mind. She was able to push it back from a May wedding to August though.

It was T-minus two-ish months before their big day. Frank gave us the berating of a lifetime because we still didn't have our suits picked out. She said Brian had been fitted for his shirt and pants already and he wasn't even a part of the wedding party. We tried to explain that it didn't really matter since we weren't getting fitted for anything fancy but she insisted that we "get our asses in gear before she kicked them."

We were to find a day in June that we happened to both be free so we decided to take advantage of it before we incurred Frank's wrath. When Keith pulled into my driveway, I kissed Mom on the forehead after checking and double-checking that she had everything she needed. She was getting pale again and they had changed some of her treatments, so I wasn't sure what kind of side effects to expect.

When I opened his passenger car door, an avalanche of soda bottles and energy drink cans spilled out. I didn't understand how any one human could survive that kind of caffeine consumption.

"Sorry man." He took a couple armfuls of garbage and put it in the backseat."

"Dude. Clean out your car." Cans and bottles crunched on the floor when I got in.

"Yeah, yeah. I will at some point."

"How much of this is from one day?"

"Two of those big energy drink cans are from breakfast. I get them and a pack of cigarettes every morning from the gas station by the house. Then I usually have a twenty-ounce pop at lunch and another energy dink if I'm feeling sluggish in the afternoon."

"You drink water at dinner?"

"About half a two liter of pop."

"Seriously, dude. That's not healthy."

"You sound like Suzanne. She keeps telling me I'm going to have a heart attack. Doctor says other than my weight I'm fine."

"I think you need to get a second opinion."

"That's exactly what Suz said. Are you going to keep riding my ass about my drinking habits or are we going to find something to wear before Frank starts up again?"

"Let's go." I shifted and more bottles and cans crunched.

We ended up at some off-rack suit place. Suzanne's dad was footing the bill so she told us to get something "that looks nice but won't bankrupt Dad."

We walked in and Keith pulled a piece of fabric out of his pocket.

"What's that?"

He rolled his eyes. "Frank gave it to me. She said 'this is satin. This is what your tie is supposed to be made of and get a real black shirt; dark grey is not close enough.'" His imitation of Frank's voice was awful.

I laughed and pulled one of those paint sample cards out of my wallet. "'This shade of purple for your shirt and Keith's tie. Not something close. This shade!'" My imitation of Frank wasn't much better.

We both laughed. "She really doesn't trust us to get this right, does she?"

"Not even a little."

"What is it about women and weddings?"

Marie Joseph-Charles 111

I was holding the swatch up to a tie. "Suzanne isn't obsessing over it."

He looked up from the clothing rack he was thumbing through. "Are you kidding? She is FREAKING OUT. I'm used to her being unglued but I think her doctor upped her meds and she's not telling me. I got up for work the other morning and she had pictures of flowers cut out of magazines and flower books with marked pages all over the kitchen table. She hadn't come to bed. She was up ALL NIGHT fussing over flowers. I tried to tell her it didn't matter because they were going to die anyway and she started crying."

"Why would you say something like that?"

"I was trying to make her feel better."

"You told a woman who is a sleep deprived walking ball of anxiety that something she thinks is important is going to die. What the fuck did you think that was going to accomplish?"

"When you say it like that it sounds stupid."

"And insensitive."

"Look, I only meant that she should get what she liked and not worry about spending her dad's money or what Frank would like since no matter what it was going to end the same way."

I shook my head at him. "Where are you taking her for the honeymoon?"

"We really can't afford much and she won't let me spend the money on something big-ish that we could afford."

"Doesn't answer my question."

"Three days in Chicago."

"Really? She doesn't really like cities."

"No but she doesn't think a cabin is camping and I won't stay in a tent. Besides, she loves museums and zoos and there are plenty of those."

"True."

"Not to mention some of the best food in the country."

There it is. That's why he wants to go. An hour later we decided we weren't going to find what Frank was looking for there and tried a different store.

We were flipping through more racks. "Did Brian ask you to be part of him and Frank's wedding?" He didn't look up.

"No. Why?"

"Just wondering. It kind of feels weird not to be part of her big day, you know?"

"Yeah, but I get it. We haven't known Brian as long or hang out with him much. Besides, you get along better with him than I do. I'm not part of your little sports club."

"We just argue about teams."

"Still. I don't talk to him as much as you do. Besides, he has four older brothers to be his groomsman."

"Yeah. Suzanne said there are going to be five bridesmaids. I wonder who his fifth will be."

"Are you going to apply for the position?"

"No. Just wondering out loud."

"Good 'cause I'm pretty sure his friend from college is his best man. I think Megan said his name is Alan or Alex or something like that."

"Adam. He's told me about him."

"I wonder if Frank's brother or sister will be there."

"Fat chance. They weren't there for her growing up. Why would they be now?"

"You would think people would just grow up. It's not Frank's fault her dad and their mom got a divorce."

"Yeah. Not like my family. Mom cheated with Dan and when Dad found out, he left. Mom married Dan and Dad moved on. I did get a decent step brother out of it though. I may not like Jackie but Dad loves her and Cody is pretty cool."

"How come you didn't ask him to be your best man?"

Keith was holding a shirt up to himself and trying to see if the sleeves were long enough. He looked at me. "Do you not want to be my best man?"

"Dude, no. It's not that. I just thought you would want family. Suzanne doesn't have a sister or anything so I get why Frank is her maid of honor but I thought you would want Cody to be part of your wedding."

He put his hand on my shoulder. "Cody's awesome but you are more of a brother to me than he is."

That kind of made me feel better. I had always thought of me, Keith, and Frank as our own little fucked up family and hearing him say that really brought those feelings back.

"Thanks." I put my hand on top of his. "You do know that shirt isn't black though. Right?"

He looked at the shirt. I held up the pants I had picked out. The shirt was about three shades lighter. "Damn it."

At the third store we had to walk through the women's lingerie to get to the nicer guy's clothes.

Keith stopped and picked up a red silk and feathery looking set that looked pretty gaudy. "She would look so sexy in this. Think I should get it for her for a wedding present?"

No, she wouldn't, I thought. "That's not a gift for her. That'd be a gift for yourself." A pink and black lace thing caught my eye. I picked it up. This on the other hand…

"Sorry man. You're girl's a redhead. I'm pretty sure there's some kind of unwritten rule about gingers wearing pink." Keith clapped my back.

Oh, yeah. Megan. "Uh. Yeah. I think you're right." I hung it back up.

We picked through more clothes in the men's department. "Why did she have to pick such difficult colors?" Keith was getting cranky. He hated shopping.

"Black and purple aren't that complicated."

"But why does it have to be so specific?"

"She just wants you to match her dress and me to match Frank."

"I haven't even seen the dress."

"You're not supposed to. It's bad luck."

"Have you seen it?"

"Yes."

"Is all of this going to be worth it?"

"What do you mean?"

"Is she going to be hot in it?"

"Really? Shouldn't you be more worried about her being happy?"

"Of course I am but I would have been happy just signing something at the court house. I'd better get something out of this"

"You get to be the center of attention for the day."

"No. The bride is the center of attention at a wedding."

"You really think Suz is going to be able to handle a lot of fuss?"

"If she takes enough of her meds, she'll be fine."

I had a horrible thought. "Are you marrying her just because you think she's hot?"

"What the fuck, man? Of course not. We take care of each other and we balance each other out. We're a good team."

That was not the answer he was supposed to give, but it was better than him saying yes to her being a trophy wife. He could have at least said he loved her.

Now I'm a Tillman: Suzanne

August 5, 2011 we had a SIMPLE ceremony. I didn't want all of the flash-and-dazzle that Frank did. Our venue was the sculpture park outside of the city. It was great because the park provided planners who took care of almost everything. All I had to take care of were the flowers, cake, and the clothes and that was more than stressful enough.

I quite unwisely put Keith in charge of the music. He was complaining that Frank and I were making all of the decisions. It seemed like the safest thing to give him control over even though he had horrible taste in music. My aunt Victoria made a beautiful three layer cake. Each layer was a different flavor- chocolate, white, and red velvet- and she iced it with homemade butter cream. I didn't ask her to make roses (she hates making roses) but she did make sugar doves for the top. It had taken a lot of work, but we did find a beautiful purple flowing dress that made Frank look like flower petal. She was my maid of honor and lone bride's maid. Ian was Keith's best man and only groomsman. We were doing this wedding on a budget and I hated fuss and fancy anyway.

I wore a mostly black dress. That was my one stipulation that I fought everyone on. I was not pure so white wasn't right and, in truth, I felt like a piece of me was dying anyway. More importantly, I wanted to wear THIS dress. My aunt Dorinda had made it for me when I was a teenager and it still fit. It was purple satin with a black lace overlay that let the purple peek through. I loved that dress and this was the perfect reason to wear it again. She had taken care of me when I was a kid along with her own daughters while my mother was away and it felt like a great way to honor her.

We had a makeshift fitting room in the park. Frank and Megan helped me get ready and we did each other's hair and makeup. They each showed up with a giant bag of makeup and skin care products. They dumped them onto the counter tops in a great cluttered mess. God knows I can't paint my own face to save my life, but Megan was able to use a brush and a little magic and turned me into something close to a work of art. Frank pulled my hair back tight against my head and twisted bits here and there. At the end, there were a hundred bobby pins poking my scalp and half a gallon of hairspray holding me together. With some measure of difficulty, I was able to wrangle Frank's hair into something somewhat befitting her amazing beauty and Megan worked her magic on her face. I really couldn't afford to hire professionals to come in and I wasn't going to let my dad pay for it. Besides, it seemed pointless to spend so much for just two people. Standing and looking in the mirror, I realized that we really didn't need professionals anyway. They gathered everything they felt wouldn't be needed for emergency touch-ups back into their bags and Megan went to join the rest of the guests.

Our outdoor ceremony was rained out. It's supposed to be good luck to have rain on your wedding day. Ha! We instead were wed in the tent we had set up for the reception. Everyone sat at their tables instead of benches in the grass.

It felt as if things were going wrong left and right on a day that I was already stressed about. Frank kept telling me everything was going to be okay. I couldn't stop pacing and cracking my knuckles. Finally, she disappeared and returned with a shot glass of tequila. She didn't have to tell me twice. At that point I didn't care if I was mixing liquor with my meds. They weren't helping me anyway. She looked me up and down and ran off, only to return with another shot. Down the gullet. I heard the music change to Canon in D and I felt like I was going to faint.

The assistants the park had provided pulled us into position. Ian squeezed my hand before taking his place next to Frank to escort her down the isle. I watched them march. Frank was visibly smiling, even from the back. Ian tugged her along. When they took their positions— Frank next to the podium and Ian next to Keith—everyone stood and turned to face me.

A wedding is supposed to be the highlight of a young girl's life. Most girls spend hundreds of thousands of hours in their lives dreaming of future husbands and beautiful gowns. Why, then, did I feel despair and dread? I was surrounded by those who loved me most. I was adorned in my most beautiful dress and the nicest jewels that we could afford. Yet, as I passed by my loved ones, down a red carpet laid out just for me, I found myself forcing a smile.

Marie Joseph-Charles 117

I looked over at my Dad on my arm. He was beaming brightly. His proud moment had finally arrived. I looked at Ian. His smile looked forced and that just made me more depressed. I looked at my future husband and felt like a hog being led to slaughter. It was if I could feel the pieces of me he is planning to cut away, leaving me an empty carcass of a wife. He had already changed so much in the time we had been together. Not all of it had been for the better. Would things continue to get worse? If felt my grip tightening on my bouquet of Casablanca lilies.

Daddy kissed my cheek and set my hand in Keith's. He gave me a reassuring smile and grinned approvingly at Keith before he sat down. As Keith and I stood and looked at each other, I felt every emotion at once. It could have been nerves or mixing straight liquor with my meds. I'm still not sure which. I do know at some point, looking at him and the confident grin he had, I started to feel a little at ease. He was so sure of all of it. He *knew* we were right for each other and he didn't question it. His confidence started to move into me until I heard "I now pronounce you Mr. and Mrs. Tillman!" I don't even remember saying "I do." I heard the words "Mr. and Mrs. Tillman" followed by a thunder of cheers and applause and suddenly I had to fight the urge to vomit so I could kiss my husband. Husband.

We left the tent and went back to the changing rooms. Tequila burns when vomited. I haven't touched it since my wedding. Thankfully, I missed my dress. What was wrong with me? Keith wasn't a bad man. He was faithful and loyal. Sure, he was a complete slob and didn't have the best hygiene and didn't always listen to me and could be a bit possessive… What marriage doesn't have difficulty?

When we could hear the DJ announce the bridal party entrance, all comforting thoughts left me. I vomited again. Frank did her best to fix me up before we met the men back at the tent entrance. Frank and Ian entered first. Frank was glowing like any happy, sister/maid of honor. Ian entered arm in arm with her and waived and blew a kiss to Megan in the crowd.

Then it was our turn. We walked in and everyone stood and cheered. He held up my hand as if to show everyone his prize. That was it. I was no longer Suzanne Elizabeth Marshall. I was now Mrs. Keith Tillman. I put on my best smile and waved to my family and friends. Keith swung me around in front of him and kissed me hard. I suddenly heard Whitney Houston's *I Will Always Love You.* We took our first dance as husband and wife and I felt myself tripping over his feet. It was not at all graceful and all eyes were on us. I was in a raging panic. Not only was everyone watching me clumsily fumbling over the dance floor, but our first dance as newly weds was to a song about breaking up.

We took our seats at the head table and appetizers were served. The DJ walked over and handed Keith a microphone. He stood and tapped his glass. "Today is the best day of my life! This beautiful woman is finally officially mine and I couldn't be happier. I've waited a long time to make Suzanne my co-driver and I know that, with her by my side, the next fifty or even seventy years will be amazing. I'm the luckiest guy in the world! I love you babe!"

He pulled me to my feet, kissed me hard again, and handed me the microphone. Dear God, I hate talking in front of people. I looked around the room. I knew there were only fifty three people there, but it felt like five hundred. I suddenly forgot the speech I had prepared. They were all staring at me and I started to panic. I gripped the microphone tighter. Frank, who was sitting to my left, gently nudged my leg under the table and nodded at me. She could read me like a book.

I cleared my throat. "Thank you all for sharing this special day with us. Keith and I are very lucky to be surrounded by so many people who care about us. It feels weird to hear the words 'husband and wife' but it feels wonderful." I was lying through my teeth. "I'm glad you will all continue to be a part of our lives together in the years to come." I sat down quickly and handed the mic to Frank.

She stood and smiled so hard, I thought her makeup would crack. "Okay. So I'm taking full credit for today!" Everyone laughed. "I love these two so much. They are family to me. I'm so glad that a few years ago they met over a simple family dinner at Mom and Dad's. Now look at them! Their lives are bound together forever." I felt like someone stabbed me in the gut when I heard the word 'forever.' Frank started crying. "It's so beautiful to see people who love each other so much come together." She started crying harder and handed the microphone over to Ian.

Ian's speech was longer but it really hit me hard. It just solidified our friendship in so many ways.

After speeches, dinner was served. I'm not sure what the seasoning on the chicken was, but it wasn't half bad. I do have to say, that I liked being served for once. All through the evening, people made their way up to the table to congratulate us. Keith's biological dad took him out of the tent for a smoke. They weren't that far behind me and I caught the words "don't fuck this up" over the music.

Suzanne and Keith's Wedding: by Ian

I remember my sister's wedding. I was a groomsman (at
her command) and she was a princess for the day. She was giddy
and smiling all day. Her life's ambition was becoming realized.
Suzanne's wedding could not have been more opposite. I was
happy to be a part of their big day but I got the impression that
Suzanne didn't feel the same way. I've never seen a bride look
more like a hostage on her wedding day. I tried to smile
reassuringly at her but I don't think it worked. Truthfully, part of
me hoped Wes would break through the tent when they got to the
'if anyone knows why these two should not be married' part just to
save her.

Compared to Frank and my sister's weddings, it was pretty
small. There probably weren't any more than fifty people there. I
don't think Suzanne's anxiety could have handled more than that.
I'm pretty sure she was a little intoxicated when she went down the
isle and through the reception she pretty much always had a wine
glass with her.

When I met her at the entrance to the tent to escort Frank
down the isle, Suz didn't look like herself at all. Part of the
problem was the makeup. She was caked in it and the silver eyelid
stuff made her look clownish. But through all of it, she looked
sick. Like I said, I'm pretty sure she had been drinking but that
wasn't it. I squeezed her hand to let her know it was going to be
okay. I don't think it helped much.

It wasn't until later, like *years* later, looking back at their
wedding video that I noticed they never really looked each other in
the eye. When they were facing each other during the ceremony,
he looked like he had just found the prize in a cereal box and she
looked like someone with Stockholm syndrome. They were all
smiles and kisses during the reception but it wasn't real. During
the first-dance-as-husband-and-wife, they didn't stand very close
to each other. I might be reading more into it than there really was
but I didn't notice much that night until it was time for speeches.

Keith's speech was all about how he was a lucky guy and
he had waited a long time to make Suzanne officially his. That
kind of bugged me a little. She wasn't a possession. Didn't he tell

Marie Joseph-Charles 121

me a few months before that they were a team? Suzanne's speech
was more of "thank you for coming" than the "this is the happiest
day of my life" that most bride's speeches are. Frank's speech was
all about how happy she was that two of her best friends were
sharing a life and she was so happy to have made it possible blah
blah blah.

I had written and rehearsed my all-important Best Man
Speech at least a hundred times. When I stood up, Suzanne was
looking at me and smiling. It was the first real smile I had seen
from her all night. Then I looked at Keith. He was leaning behind
Suz and Frank to say something to Brian. Screw my speech. Let's
wing this shit.

"Keith. I could tell an embarrassing story or two from us
growing up together like most best men do but there are just too
many to choose from. You're an idiot and you've done A LOT of
stupid things." Keith sat forward to pay attention. I looked at
Suzanne and she was still smiling at me. "But it looks like you
may have finally done something smart. You now have a wife—I
never thought I would say those words—who is smart, beautiful,
funny and successful. She is your polar opposite in every way.
And luckily for you, opposites attract and by the grace of GOD
you were smart enough not to screw this up." Everyone was
laughing but only Frank and Suzanne seemed to realize I wasn't
entirely joking. "Suzanne, if he doesn't do everything in his power
to make you the happiest woman on Earth, let me know. I'll kill
him myself." More laughter at my not-joking joke. "I want
nothing but happiness for you both. Congratulations." There was
a lot of cheering and clinking glasses. Keith stood up and shook
my hand. He was laughing and completely oblivious to the fact
that I meant what I said about him treating her right.

Suzanne hugged me. "Thank you."

I pulled back and looked her in the eye. "I mean it."

"I know." She smiled and squeezed my hand before she sat
back down.

Megan pulled me over to her and kissed my cheek.
"You're such a good guy."

I kissed her hand and looked her in the eye. "I know."

Graduation Bonfire: by Suzanne

I'm still not sure how I survived my senior year of Vet School. Most of my twenty-plus hour days are a caffeine-fueled blur. Since school was so far away, I didn't always make it home. The truck stop became my sanctuary. Cheap coffee and a safe place to sleep in my car were my primary survival needs. Keith and I talked on the phone every chance we could in the beginning, but that faded over time. Often it was just a text message here and there. Switching from early mornings of sixteen hour days for my surgery rotation to fourteen hour third-shift nights made things difficult and probably damaged my sanity a little.

Things were further complicated by the fact that I didn't usually want to go home. I missed Ariel and, to some extent, Keith but he made things difficult. He was one of those men who was a perpetual sixteen-year-old boy. He preferred to live in his own mess rather than take time from hobbies because it was easier and he wholly believed that being an adult was about paying bills and little else. The several times a week I made it home, I was greeted by a mountain of dirty dishes. He had car parts and other random objects strewn around the living room. Laundry in the bedroom made a new carpet on the floor. He swore it was separated by clean and dirty but in the mornings I often saw him doing the sniff test. When you have a diagnosed anxiety disorder coupled with a form a depression, coming into that after days of insomnia fueled by adrenaline and caffeine, everything just feels worse.

I know he didn't mean to make things hard on me. The facts were simple; he didn't understand my messed up brain and he didn't care that he made it worse. I felt selfish when I brought it up and asked him to clean up after himself and he would tell me he was tired of being attacked. I wasn't the only one who had long, hard days and I needed to understand his needs and since we shared the house, he had a say in how it was kept too. Sometimes I felt like the only reason he was happy I came home was so that I could scoop the cat box.

I don't want you to get the wrong impression of him. He's not all asshole. I came home once after having been awake for four days straight. He took one look at me, drew me hot oatmeal and lavender bath, and brought me a cup of chamomile tea while I soaked. I passed out cold in under ten minutes. He got me out of the water, dried me off, and put me to bed. Another time, I came home to a bouquet of carnations on the kitchen table for no discernable reason. I hate carnations, but I appreciated the gesture.

It was all worth it on the last day in spring of 2012 when I ran to my car. I stopped by the truck stop to say goodbye to the friends I had made there and I headed home for good! I still had to study for the NAVLE but that could wait for now. A week after I completed, Frank finished her stretch at Purdue and, of course, there was a party.

Cathy insisted that we had to celebrate properly and held a bonfire in the back yard with enough liquor and kegs to start her own bar. I didn't like the idea of such a loud and large group of people but I knew she wouldn't take 'no' for an answer. Frank's cousin stood at the gate and collected everyone's keys (unless they were the designated driver) as we filed in. I saw Ian and Megan meandering around but it was several hours before I could talk to either of them.

About three hours into the evening, Keith started his usual crap. Whenever he was around friends or groups, he turned into this loud, obnoxious jerk. He exaggerated stories (like that he had to save me from drowning in the bathtub when I fell asleep) and made a few snide jabs at my weight. It didn't take long for me to have enough and I quietly backed away and ducked out of the group.

I waddled down the hill and found a nice spot near the trees. I lay down in the damp grass. I breathed deep the cool-earthy air. It was refreshing after standing near the bonfire and Keith's smoking. I looked up at the stars. It felt like it had been ages since I'd seen the night sky. I took another deep breath. I could feel the tension slowly seeping away from me and into the ground. I closed my eyes and breathed again.

I'm not sure how long I was laying there before I heard, "Whatcha doin'?"

I opened my eyes and saw Ian's lean frame standing over me. I closed my eyes again. "Soaking into the ground."

"Want some company?"

"Sure."

He lay down in the grass with the top of his head touching the top of mine. "You do know this party is for you, right?"

"And Frank."

"True but it's not really normal for the guest of honor to be hiding from her own party."

"I just needed to get away for a few."

"You don't like lots of people. Why did you agree to a party?"

"Have you ever tried to say 'no' to Cathy?"

"Once. It didn't go the way I wanted. I see your point."

"Besides. It's not so much the group right now. It's really just one person in the group."

"Keith being Keith?"

"Yeah. It's like he has this jerk alter ego that comes out when he's around other people."

"He's kind of always been like that."

"That doesn't mean I have to like it."

"This is true. Are you at least glad to be done with school?"

I felt myself smile. "Yes!" I threw my hands up towards the stars.

He laughed

"What's going on here?" I turned my head slightly and saw Keith coming down the hill.

Ian looked at him too. "It's called a conversation, dude."

Keith ignored him and looked at me. "I was wondering where you went. I looked over and you weren't standing next to me anymore so I came to look for you."

"I'm fine." I pushed myself up and stood. "I just needed some fresh air."

"That anxiety stuff again?"

I felt a twinge of annoyance. "Yeah."

Just then, Megan came stumbling down the hill. She was clearly HEAVILY intoxicated and a giggling mess. "I found you!"

Ian shook his head. "I think we had better get you home."

"No no no no no. I don't want to go home!"

"You are way to drunk to keep drinking."

"Oh! That's a hard one! You are way to drink to keep drunking." She mimicked his voice and burst into laughter.

"Come on. You can sleep in my bed." He picked her up and threw her over his shoulder.

"Woohoo! I'm getting lucky tonight! I feel like a cavewoman!" She cackled as he headed back up the hill and across the street.

I smiled and shook my head. They were a cute couple but I couldn't help but feel a little bit of jealousy.

Life's Prize: by Ian

Keith and I were hanging out in his garage one day a little less than a year after the wedding. He'd taken off his ring and put it in his pocket. I was pretty sure any woman other than Suzanne would have had a fit about that.

He had his hand in the engine bay of the Corvair and I was sitting on the work bench. "Being married hasn't changed things too much. At least now I can say she's legally mine."

I hated when he talked about Suz like he owned her. "Uh huh." That was about all I could say that wasn't going to start an argument.

"What about you and Megan?"

"What about us?"

"Me and Suz are married. Frank's getting married soon. That just leaves you two."

"Yeah. I don't think we are ready for that."

"Why not?"

"We are still just broke college students barely making ends meet. We've got other things to worry about."

"You are focusing on the wrong stuff."

"What do you mean?" I picked up a torque wrench and handed it to him.

He wiped his hand with a red rag and took it from me. "College will be over at some point. You aren't getting any younger and you have a pretty woman who loves you."

"I like to think of Megan as more than a pretty face."

"That's right. You're an ass man."

"Dude. I'm being serious."

"Me too. You're my brother. We grew up together. I want to see you settled down and happy like me."

"Who says I'm not happy?" I kind of felt a little attacked.

He looked at me. "You've worked hard. You've played this game of life. Now it's time to ask yourself if you want that prize. You've earned the right to be happy with Megan."

I knew what he was trying to say but he was doing it all wrong.

Marie Joseph-Charles 128

"Maybe someday we will but it's not going to happen now. Besides, I would want to give her the wedding she deserves and I financially I can barely take her to dinner and a movie."

"Start saving. Me and Suz only spent about five grand but, last count, I heard Frank was up over fifteen."

"Holy shit."

"You know Cathy. She'd rather go bankrupt that see Frank go without."

"Still though."

He handed the wrench back to me. "Seriously. Just think about it, man."

"Yeah yeah."

It's not that I hadn't thought about moving forward with Megan but I did feel marriage was much too fast. Even with as much time as we spent together, we didn't really know each other. When we were together, we were usually studying or talking about school. Sometimes we could catch a basketball or football game together. That wasn't much. Come to think of it, I couldn't even say what her favorite food was. Nope. No marriage. Not now.

That night I was sitting at dinner with Megan. I told her what Keith had said.

"But someday you want to get married, right?" She was twirling pasta on her fork but looking straight at me.

"I mean, yeah, I guess. But not now. I'm lucky I can pay for that spaghetti you're eating, let alone give you the wedding you deserve."

She kind of smiled and sat up. "You know, I wouldn't want anything extravagant. And traditionally, it would be my family paying for it anyway."

"Can't get you a ring, either."

"That wouldn't have to be fancy either."

I suddenly wished I hadn't brought it up. "Someday maybe."

She looked hurt and I suddenly felt like a big dick. Truthfully, if I had felt more confident with where we were, I probably would have been okay saying yes, I would marry her someday. But, like I said, I didn't know as much about her as I should have. I didn't know her favorite music. Suzanne liked to listen to Native American flutes if she was painting but her favorite band was Linkin Park when she thought no one could see her dancing in her living room. I didn't know Megan's favorite animal. Frank's were those yappy little Maltese dogs. I didn't know Megan's favorite book. Suzanne's was Lord of the Flies.

Keith wasn't all wrong. I did work hard in life and Megan did make me happy. Maybe she was a reward from the powers that be. Who knows? I just didn't think we were there yet and I really felt like an ass for bringing it up and then shooting her down.

Clifty Falls: by Suzanne

After vet school, Frank found work in Indianapolis so that Brian wouldn't have to change jobs. They moved from their shoebox to a nice two-story with a finished basement and, of course, a white picket fence. I stayed right where I was. The emergency clinic where I had cut my teeth on veterinary medicine offered me a job as a vet (after I passed my boards) working two regular fourteen hour shifts a week and then let me fill in for any vet that wanted off. There were six other veterinarians and they all had lives and families. There were always shifts to fill.

Life was still busy, but a little less crazy. Ian kept his word and made time to spend a day at Clifty Falls with me in July. Keith was not at all happy about the idea of me running around the forest with another man. He looked a little sheepish when I pointed out that it was his best friend and if he truly didn't trust him, he was the problem, not Ian.

At 7am, I heard Ian's car pull up in the driveway. I grabbed my little knapsack and flung it over my shoulder. I kissed Ariel on top of the head and told him to be a good boy while I was away. I waved to Keith and told him to have a good day at work. He was sitting at the kitchen table with a bowl of cold cereal. He somewhat grudgingly told me to be careful and enjoy my day.

I ran out the front door and almost didn't open the car door before trying to get in.

He smiled at me. "A little excited?"

I was pretty much bouncing in the passenger seat. "Maybe a little."

We stopped for coffee and cinnamon rolls to carbo-load before our long day. The whole morning I was excitedly (and probably annoyingly) chattering away. All through breakfast and the almost two hour drive, I just would not shut up. It was weird. I'm normally pretty quiet but I just couldn't contain my excitement that morning.

We could not have asked for a more perfect day. The sun was warm, bright, and full. Clouds were few and far between. And, best of all, it was a Monday so we basically had the park to ourselves.

Marie Joseph-Charles 131

We took trail one down to trail two. For those of you who have never been, trail two is the riverbed. It's rugged and unkempt. If a tree falls over, you find a way over or under it. The water is up? You're going to get wet. By the way, I hope you don't mind snakes because on a warm, sunny day just after hatching season, they are under virtually every rock. After a little over two hours, Ian found a baby bird on the ground.

He looked down at the helpless little fledgling that was paralyzed with fear. "Well, sorry little buddy. I guess you're snake food now."

The biologist in me knew he was right- circle of life and all of that. But the human woman in me- the one who looked down and saw a helpless baby animal- knew she had to help. I looked up and saw a nest a little over twenty feet up on an overhanging tree branch.

"I'll bet he came from up there." I pointed at the nest.

He looked up. "It's a miracle he didn't splat on impact."

I shook my head. It was a fledgling. It had some feathering so it had probably slowed its own decent. "We need to get him back up there."

"Won't a mother animal reject its babies if it smells humans?"

I laughed. "First of all, most birds have a horrible sense of smell. Second, that's a crock. A hundred years ago a mother told her son that so he wouldn't kidnap defenseless baby animals and bring them home. It's been passed on through the generations and now accepted as fact."

"Okay, then." He looked back up at the nest. "How do we get it back up there?"

"That's the easy part. Gimme your boot."

"Use your own damn boot. What are you going to do? Throw it up there like a football?"

"I can't climb the tree with only one boot."

"You think you're going to climb that?"

"Yes. Now give me your boot."

He sat down on a rock and pulled off his left boot. "It better not shit in there."

I tucked the little chick safely down deep in the boot and secured it to my belt with the laces. "Now give me a boost."

He rolled his eyes. "You're going to fall and break your neck and I'm going to have to explain to Keith that you died trying to rescue snake food." He laced his fingers together for me to step into.

I placed my hands on his quite-muscular shoulders to steady myself. I barely had time to pick a part of the lowest branch to aim for before he had hoisted me up. For a split second I felt like I had gone a little airborne but I caught the branch I swung my legs up (just missing kicking his face) and threw my right leg over the branch. I rocked a little and the rest of my body followed until I was sitting upright on the branch. The shoe dangled with the heavy sole facing the ground the whole time; never losing the precious little feathered cargo inside. I stood up and pulled myself up onto the next branch and then the next.

When I finally reached the branch the nest was sitting on, I discovered I had two problems. Problem one: If I moved too far from the trunk, there was no way the branch would hold my weight. Problem two: The nest was just out of arm's reach. I looked down at Ian. He was looking up at me and even through his sunglasses I could tell he had that shit-she's-going-to-fall look on his face. I detached the boot from my belt. I straddled the branch and carefully and slowly inched my way out as close to the nest as I could. When I felt the branch start to bend under me, I stopped. I reached out as far as I could while holding the boot by the toe. I carefully turned it and dumped the little tweeter out and into the safety of his nest.

I heard applause below me and I startled. I slipped a little and dropped the boot.

"Hey!" I saw him hobble over to retrieve it.

"Sorry!" I carefully backed to the trunk and began lowering myself carefully branch by branch. When I was back to the lowest one, I looked down at him. "You're going to have to help me down."

"This is not going to end well." He reached up to help me.

I wish I could say this was some kind of romantic movie. I wish I could say that I swung down into his arms gracefully and he lowered me down the length of his body until my feet touched the ground. That his strong arms held me securely. That, when our eyes met, we knew some kind of magic. But real life isn't a romantic movie. In reality, he was right. It didn't end well. Instead of a poetic descent, I lost my grip. I was a cartoon anvil that came crashing down on his head. We both hit the creek bed hard.

"Oh my God! Are you okay?!" I was scrambling to get off him.

He was laughing. He was laughing too hard to speak.

"I'm so sorry. Oh my God. I'm so sorry."

He stood up, still laughing. "It's okay. I'm squishy enough. It absorbed most of the impact."

I felt a little better after he said that. The truth was, he had very little squish to him and I felt like I had landed on one of the boulders.

We hiked a little further up and then headed up the side of the cliff. We found a nice overlook and stopped to snack on jerky and almonds.

"You think little Snake Food will be okay?" He wasn't looking at me. He was looking back down the direction we had come from.

I looked over at him. I have to admit, a black t-shirt, mirrored aviators, and a little compassion looked damn good on him. "He will be now."

"Good."

Frank's wedding: By Suzanne

Frank's wedding was everything you would expect and more. It's amazing how she and her mom were able to pull together such a massive affair with such a small budget (according to the wedding coordinator it was small). She had her four female cousins and me as bridesmaids. I couldn't have scraped together five bridesmaids for my wedding if my life had depended on it. I was grateful that we were able to talk her out of the horrid pink dresses and into a tasteful shade of blue. I'd much rather look like a blueberry than cotton candy.

The morning of September 15, 2012, we were up at 5a.m. to start "the process." Who knew church basements could be so versatile? Manicures, pedicures, professional hair stylists, mimosas… it was a chaotic, champagne-charged escapade. I've never felt so much like a doll. Every part of my body was tucked, sucked, glued, or painted. The end result was five perfectly decorated Persian blue princesses and one fabulously bejeweled snow queen.

We did a final mirror check before taking our places upstairs. Frank had been very clear with the makeup artists that she didn't want any of us "looking like clowns." She wanted us to look as natural as possible. But, as I looked in the mirror, I didn't really recognize the face looking back. I never wore makeup so I had no idea I could look this… not plain. There wasn't a pimple or scar to be seen. The dark circles under my eyes were virtually undetectable. I didn't have much time to decide if I liked this look as we were ushered upstairs by the coordinator.

The original procession had me immediately following Beverly, Frank's maid of honor. I had insisted on being the last bridesmaid because "family first." In reality, I wanted to be as far away from where the cameras would be pointed as possible.

In one of the videos, you can hear Ian say, "Jesus Christ. She's beautiful" when Frank steps into the doorway behind me. She really did look beautiful. Head to toe she looked like every little girl's dream. The stylist had done her long blonde hair in some kind of magical updo with most of the sides sleeked against her head and her face framed in golden curls cascading down from the tiara that held her nose-length veil. The makeup artist really did her natural beauty justice. Her eyes looked bluer, her cheekbones looked higher, and there was not a freckle or blemish to be seen. Her sleeveless white dress fitted her form (and contained her boobs) elegantly and had a fifteen foot train fastened at the back with two jeweled butterflies that matched our dresses. The fake rocks around her neck glittered and could have easily passed for real, though I doubt anyone was looking at her throat. Her feet (that no one could see) were comfortably fitted in brand new white sneakers that she had swapped the laces for actual lace and bejeweled the sides to match her necklace because she was still Frank under all of the silk and makeup.

When Brian saw her, he looked like he had just won the lottery. He stood straight, tall, and proud as she walked towards him and their eyes remained locked throughout the ceremony. I remember feeling a little sad that Keith hadn't looked at me like that. And, I have to add, I was proud of Frank for not fainting or vomiting from all of the champagne we'd had that morning.

"Do you, Francesca Eloise Napolitano…" Frank winced at hearing her full name. She hated her name. "…take Brian to be your husband? Do you promise to love him, trust him, and care for him in sickness and in health until death do you part?"

Her eyes sparkled a little. She was trying not to cry. "I do."

"Do you Brian Alexander Calloway take Francesca to be your wife? Do you promise to love her, trust her, and care for her in sickness and in health until death do you part?"

He puffed out his chest at his big moment. "I do."

Just like that. A two word answer and an exchange of jewelry and they just promised in front of three hundred people and recording cameras that they would be together forever. No hesitation. They knew in their hearts that this was forever. Why was I so incapable of that kind of certainty? Was there something wrong with me? Was there something wrong with them in that they had such blind faith?

As soon as the minister said "Kiss the bride," Frank jumped into Brian's arms and threw her arms around his neck. It was a beautiful moment and I couldn't stop smiling for her.

After the ceremony, there was another two hours of photographs at the park by the river. We were starving but thankfully most of Frank's cousins were moms and they were able to pool the contents of their purses for a microfeast of beef jerky, goldfish crackers, and fruit snacks.

When we finally made it to the reception venue, everyone was already there and seated. Servers walked around with little trays of spinach filled pastries and some kind of tartar looking vegetable substance on a cracker. The coordinator rushed up to a microphone stand and announced us all in our procession pairs. I was uncomfortable with so many eyes on me. It had been easier to ignore at the church; probably because no one was applauding then. I took my seat at the head table and Keith came up to join me.

He smiled. "You look good."

That was it. FIVE HOURS of grooming and primping and getting my face painted and all I got was, 'You look good.' I don't have words for that kind of frustration.

When Frank and Brian entered, six hundred hands clapped, at least two hundred people yelled, and there was a lot of whistling. They held each other's hand high in the air like a boxing champion as they waived. They took their seats at the head of the table and dinner was served.

After dinner, the newlyweds went to say 'hi' to their guests, the cousins went out to mingle with family and friends, the groomsmen wandered off with their wives and girlfriends, and the table emptied. Keith was easily bored and a die-hard nicotine addict so he abandoned me to go hang out outside with the other smokers. There I sat, alone at a ridiculously long table, twirling my wine glass and people watching.

Ian walked up and held out his hand. "I'm tired of sitting. Come dance with me."

I smiled. "I don't think you want to do that. I have two left feet."

"That's fine. I have two right ones. We'll even out."

I laughed. I really didn't have a response to that. Who says something like that? I shook my head and let him lead me out onto the dance floor. He held my left hand in his right and his left hand rested on my waist. His hands were huge and warm. Oh my God, he smelled good! As we danced (it was Better Together by Jack Johnson, in case you're wondering), we talked about the happy couple and speculated their future. We even made a small wager. I bet twenty dollars that the first baby would come in less than a year. He said that they were too career driven and it would be at least five.

Looking back on it now, I see a huge difference in my comfort. At my own wedding, I was a stumbling mess when I danced with Keith. A lot of that was probably just the fact that everyone was watching me. But at Franks, with Ian, I didn't notice anything off. I danced just fine. I wasn't nervous or uncomfortable. It was just us; two friends dancing at a wedding.

"Seriously?!" I heard Keith yell. I turned and he was standing behind me. His face was reddening with rage.

"What is your problem, Dude?" Ian got in between me and my furious husband.

"What are you two doing?"

"It's called 'dancing.' It's what people do at weddings." I stepped forward. I could hear the pitch in my voice elevate.

Everyone was staring at us. The music had stopped playing and I had reached a level of humiliation had never felt before. How dare he?

"If you wanted to dance, you could have just come and told me and there is no reason for you two to be that close or for him to touch you there!"

Okay. Anger was crowding out embarrassment. "First of all, you left me to go smoke, like you always do. Second, we've been together how long and you have only ONCE danced with me AND IT WAS AT OUR FUCKING WEDDING. And third, are you FUCKING KIDDING ME? It's dancing at a wedding with a friend!"

"You don't understand. He has a history-"

"History of cheating. Yeah, you've told me. Apparently, so do I by the way you act." I turned to Ian. "Thank you for the dance." I turned back to Keith. "Thank you for ruining my best friend's wedding and humiliating me."

I stormed out into the parking lot.

Marie Joseph-Charles 139

Frank's Wedding by Ian

Frank's wedding had all of the insanity you would expect. She had always strived for perfection and somehow always managed to pull it off, even if it did require a little help. I wasn't expecting her to have a church wedding. I always knew she was Christian but I never knew her to actually practice it. I think it had more to do with Brian and making his family happy.

Speaking of Brian's family… all four brothers were the groomsmen. Can I just say that the level of Déjà vu was terrifying when I saw them all arriving with their wives and girlfriends. Rob and Dylan's wives were leggy blondes just like Frank (Dylan's wife was pregnant) and Zack's girlfriend was a beautiful brunette like Suz but with makeup and fake highlights in her hair. Trevor was trying not to cry. Apparently his wife (the fiancée that kept texting him on Thanksgiving a few years prior) had left him with no warning. Rob kept telling him to "man up. You'll find a woman worthy of you someday." They had all brought their kids and left them with some other relative to run amuck in the church upstairs while they hugged Brian and then the women went back upstairs.

Brian's dad, Tony, and mom, Anna, came down to where we were in the basement to hug Brian before she went upstairs to see to last minute details and guide the photographer they had hired (separate from the one Frank hired). Surprise! Both blonde haired and blue-eyed. It was like something out of a freaky horror movie. *Aryan Paradise staring the Calloway Family.*

Adam, Brian's best man, looked like he could have been one of the Calloways. He was blonde haired but brown eyed. His wife had so many different colors streaked in her hair, I'm not sure what color it actually was. She didn't seem entirely lucid and I wondered if she was on something.

Keith and I hung out in the basement with the Calloway clan while they got dressed. Rob pulled a bottle of Wild Turkey and a bunch of shot glasses out of the duffle bag his clothes were in. Apparently, it's a thing to have a 'bourbon blessing' before a wedding or the marriage won't last. I wondered if Trevor'd had one.

Brian's dad held up his glass and we all followed suit. "It's your day, Tater Tot. You seem to have found a good woman. She takes care of business, cooks, cleans, and obeys." I almost choked on that one. Had he actually met Frank? "Soon she'll bear your sons and you'll be blessing their weddings one day. In acknowledgment of this holy purpose, and of the power of this occasion, let us pray." Everyone bowed their heads but held the glasses high. "Help Frank and Brian find the perfect place in this world for their union to flourish. May all their future creations be blessed. Amen."

All of the Calloways, "Amen." Burbon down the hole.

That was awkward and uncomfortable.

One of the wedding coordinators came down to get us all into place. There were blue flowers with white ribbons at the end of every pew and big bouquets at the alter. Whoever did the husbandry with those flowers outdid themselves. Brian was at the alter rocking on his toes. I was sitting in an isle part of the pew with Megan next to me and Keith directly in front of me in a different pew. A photographer with a video camera was partially between us in the isle.

The music changed and the church doors opened.

Tony escorted Anna. Steve escorted Cathy. Adam with Beverly. Rob with Sara. Can I just say that five members in your wedding party – not including the bride and groom - is seriously excessive? Finally, it was almost Frank's turn but before her were Suzanne and Zack. Jesus Christ, she was beautiful. I knew I shouldn't be thinking that with my girlfriend holding my hand next to me, but I couldn't help it. I also couldn't help the weird hollow feeling I had in my gut when I paid attention to how close they were walking.

Through the vows, Megan held a tight grip on my hand. She looked like she might cry any minute. I really hoped she wasn't hinting at something. I had too much going on in my life with Mom and school and just surviving day to day without even considering revisiting our marriage conversation.

'I Do's' were said. Tears were shed. And the wedding party filed out to go take pictures at the park. We were all hungry and it would be several hours before the reception. Keith, Megan, and I walked down the street to the bar for some appetizers before we went to the reception hall.

We sat at the bar and ordered pop and mozzarella sticks and onions.

"I'm so glad I'm not marrying into that family." Megan popped an onion pedal in her mouth.

Keith looked past me at her. "Why? Don't you like Brian?"

"Of course I do but I don't like his brothers and I *really* don't like the idea of dying my hair blonde."

I laughed. "You would look terrible as a blonde."

"Why don't you like his brothers?" Keith had honed in on something and, as usual, wasn't going to let it drop.

"They're all bullies and treat their wives like things."

"You're reading too much into things."

"Whatever. All I know is Trevor's wife was smart to bail."

"How did you know about Trevor's wife?"

"I'm a woman. Bathroom talk. Duh."

"It's not very nice for you to say that. Trevor's upset about it." Keith tried to defend the man.

"Then he shouldn't have called her 'useless' when she had a miscarriage."

"Whoa!" I turned to face her. "He did what?"

"She miscarried and he told her if she couldn't have children she was useless. Anna says he didn't mean it but look at the way the rest of them are."

"If Brian ever said something like that to Frank, she'd castrate him. And being a vet, she'd know how to make sure it hurt."

"I'm sure he just said it because he was upset. He's not a bad guy." Keith wouldn't let it go.

"Whatever." Megan rolled her eyes."

We snacked in relative silence until we had to go to the reception hall. It was everything you would expect from Frank. Perfect flowers. Perfect music. Good food. She wouldn't have it any other way.

Halfway through the reception, I looked up at the main table and saw Suz sitting alone. She was playing with her wine glass and looked completely let down. I leaned over to Megan. "I'm going to go cheer up Suzanne."

She looked, I don't know, disappointed maybe. "Okay," she said.

I walked up to the head table. I don't remember what I said to her. I hope it was something witty but I doubt it. What I do remember was how she lit up and smiled. It was like her mood did a complete one-eighty. I remember how small she felt when I put my hand on her waist and how soft her hand was in mine. And I remember betting her twenty bucks that it would be a few years before Brian and Frank started a family.

Most of all, I remember hearing Keith yell above the music. "Seriously?!"

I looked passed Suzanne as she turned to face him. He was red and pissed. I asked him what his problem was. Frank later told me I got in front of Suz like I was trying to shield her. I don't remember doing it but I do remember her screaming back at him and leaving in tears.

I felt like my temperature was going up; like I was going to hit that white-hot rage point. "'History of cheating'? Are you kidding me? I made a mistake in HIGH SCHOOL."

He turned to me, still red and looking like he might cry. "Cheating is cheating, man."

I'm pretty sure I was going to hit him but Megan grabbed my arm and pulled me back just as Frank marched passed me and straight up got in Keith's face. She opened her mouth to yell at him but her jaw started to shake and she burst into tears and ran passed him.

Megan was still holding my arm when Brian walked up to Keith. It was amazing how calmly and yet, so angrily said "You need to leave. Now." Keith left and Brian turned towards me. He gave me a reaffirming shoulder squeeze (which surprisingly defused me a bit) before he went after his wife.

The reception resumed but with a new conversation topic going around the guest tables. Me and Megan sat down and the waiter set a glass beer in front of me. Trevor had watched the whole thing from the open bar and told them to take me a drink. Good looking out, man.

Megan was rubbing my arm but I didn't really feel it. My hands were still fists and I was still raging pretty bad.

"You okay?" I almost didn't hear her over the music and my own pulse in my ears.

I took a deep breath and turned to her. "Yeah. I'll be fine."

"What was that 'history of cheating' thing about?"

I clenched my fists harder. I explained the whole thing with Roquel and how her boyfriend had cheated on her so she slept with me to get back at him. We were eighteen and I didn't even know she was dating someone.

"So he's mad at you because some chick almost a decade ago used you?" Her hand was on top of my fist. I think she was trying to relax it but it wasn't working.

"Apparently."

"That's stupid."

"Yup. He didn't seem that pissed at me when it happened."

"You think he doesn't trust you now?"

"Obviously!" I didn't mean to snap at her but it was too late to take it back.

"Okay. I'm going to go check on Frank. Calm yourself down." She left me at the table by myself. I downed the whole beer as I watched her walk away.

It wasn't too long later that Frank emerged from wherever she had run. She was completely composed and said something about not letting one jackass ruin the night. I found that respectable. It was a little while longer before I calmed down enough to apologize to Megan. Several of us tried to call Suzanne to check on her, but she wasn't picking up her phone. They had to do the bouquet and garter toss without her which kind of broke Frank's heart.

Keith stayed at his parents' house for something like two weeks after that. He had come home and Suzanne had left a garbage bag of his clothes on the front porch. She eventually let him back in the house but it was a while before she had forgiven him.

When Frank and Brian came back from their honeymoon in Tuscany, he was in Indy waiting for them. I think they got a better apology than Suz did. As for me? This was pretty much our conversation:

Keith: "Hey man. I'm sorry. I don't know what came over me."

Me: "Whatever."

Keith: "We good?"

Me: "No."

Keith: "Can we at least move on?"

Me: "Fine."

That was it. He just wanted to pretend it never happened. Okay. Fine. I wasn't one for drama but I was definitely still pissed. I think it was months before any of us really forgave him.

Everything Frank had always wanted: By Suzanne

It was late at night the winter after Frank's wedding. I was dead tired. A seventeen hour shift should be felonious. Granted, I'm the one who forgot I was already working and agreed to cover part of another shift… I came home and crawled into bed next to Keith. He had put on so much weight that I had to sleep on the very edge of the bed to keep from sliding down into him. I was so far in dreamland that I couldn't even hear his ridiculous snoring (which, believe me, is a feat). But there's one thing that can always wake me up. I opened my eyes. Frank was kneeling at my bedside.

"What in the actual Hell?" I pulled a pillow over my head.

"I'm sorry."

"Please tell me I'm dreaming." I didn't even move the pillow. If I looked at her again, I would have known she was really there.

"I'm sorry, Suz, but I *really* need a milkshake."

I moved the pillow. Her eyes were pleading. "Well, you drove two hours for it so let me at least put on shoes."

She looked a little relieved. "I'll wait in the living room." She left.

I looked over at Keith. He was snoring away without so much as twitch of recognition that there was an intruder in our bedroom again. Lucky asshole.

I stumbled out into the living room. I had put jeans on under my flannel nightshirt and jammed my feet into the nearest shoes I could find, not even bothering to put on socks. My hair was a mess, my breath probably could have gassed someone to death, and I just didn't care.

She looked me up and down. "Maybe I should drive."

It wasn't until we hit the bright lights inside the restaurant that it suddenly hit me. Frank wasn't wearing any makeup and her clothes didn't quite match. She wasn't the perfectly made-up Barbie doll I was used to seeing in public. This must be some serious news.

We ordered the usual and found a booth. I rubbed more of the sleep from my eyes. "Spill."

She took a deep breath. "You can't tell anyone until I figure out what I'm going to do."

"You know I respect the sanctity of anything that is said over milkshakes."

She smiled a little as our shakes were set on the table in front of us. She took a deep breath. "I know. But this time, I'm really…" She trailed off and started fiddling with her shake like she always did.

"Holy Hell. You're pregnant." I just knew. I didn't know how I knew. I just knew.

She looked at me through the tops of her eyes and they filled with tears. "Yeah."

"Why are you crying? You've always wanted to be a mother! You practically raised Keith and Ian!"

She laughed and choked the tears back. "I know. I know I should be happy. But this wasn't part of the plan. We were supposed to be more settled in our jobs and enjoy married life for a little while first."

"I'm going to guess you haven't told Brian yet."

"No. You and Keith have been together longer than we have. How did you keep from getting pregnant?"

I looked at her with a face that said something to the effect of 'you have to ask?'

"Oh."

"Celibacy has its perks."

"I'm sorry I asked."

"Don't be. He chose to kill our sex life. But that's not the issue here."

"I just don't know what to do."

"I don't know what you're asking. You're you. Termination is not an option. You're going to go home, tell Brian, and you guys are going to raise one spoiled little niece or nephew for me."

She smiled. "You make it sound so simple."

"What's difficult? You have the degree. You have the job. You have the husband. You have the house. Soon you will have the kids. These are all the things you have always wanted. Yeah, it's a little sooner than you expected, but that's life."

Marie Joseph-Charles 148

"This is why I drove two hours in the middle of the night." She smiled and reached across the table to squeeze my hand.

I yawned. "Next time you decide to pee on a stick, can you do it on a night I haven't worked a double?"

She laughed. "Sorry."

Thankfully this exchange didn't happen with every pregnancy. That night, she drove back home after we talked silly girl talk like baby names and shower ideas. I think it helped ease a little of the angst she was still having about how to break the news to Brian. I went home and passed out face first in my pillow with my jeans still on. When I woke up later in the morning, I text messaged Frank to find out if she had broken the news yet. I wanted to tell Ian he owed me twenty bucks.

Seven months later, I found myself sitting in a hospital waiting room with Ian, Megan, and Brian's family. I had dropped everything and taken off to Indiana when I got the call that she was in labor. I was going to be an Auntie! Aunties get all the fun of kids with none of the parental responsibilities! This was going to be great! I called Ian on the way to see if he wanted to ride together but he said he was picking up Megan. Megan hadn't originally planned on going but Frank had insisted that she wanted her whole family there and that included Megan.

At 10:56p.m. on July 13, 2013 a beautiful baby girl named Amber Lynn Calloway entered the world with ten fingers, ten toes, and weighing in at seven pounds and nine ounces. When Brian came out of the delivery room and announced that they had a baby girl, I jumped out of my chair and hugged him. I'm pretty sure I knocked Ian out of the way to do it.

Brian's family were shaking his hand and congratulating him. Rob said something to the effect of "better luck next time." Okay. It was a daughter instead of a son but that was still his baby. I resisted the urge to punch him in the face. Joke was on him though. They had another daughter, Christina Renee, a little over a year later in September 2014. Third time was the charm, though, when Chadwick Xavier Calloway finally arrived in April of 2016.

Keith arrived a little later. He had been tied up at work but finally made it. I filled him in. He joined me, Ian, and Megan in a game of cards while we waited to be allowed to go back and see Frank and the baby. It felt like eternity but we were finally given the okay to go back.

Frank looked exhausted but happy. Brian was sitting next to her holding her hand against his lips. At first, I loved how adoringly he looked at her. When I looked a little closer, though, his expression was more concern and maybe a little disappointment than adoration. My momentary warm, fuzzy feeling passed quickly. There was still something I didn't like about him, but he was family now.

Cathy set the baby in my arms. She was so little and pink. I liked newborns because they weren't all gross and drooly and snotty yet. I rocked gently as I looked at her. There was a little piece of maternity still inside me. There would always be a nagging voice in the back of my brain that would tell me I'm supposed to be a mother. Thankfully rationality always won when I reminded myself of all the reasons I should NOT be a mother. She yawned. Being born must be exhausting.

I passed her to Keith. He held one hand under her head and one under her body. It looked kind of like he was going to toss a little pink football. He carefully passed her to Megan.

Megan held her close and looked down at the newest Calloway. She got that look on her face. All women recognize it. That "this is what I want" look. A look of pure contentment as your subconscious starts pretending that the baby is yours and life is complete. Poor Ian. She looked at him with a huge smile.

He kissed her forehead. "Maybe some day."

She looked disheartened but happy that it wasn't a flat "no."

We stuck around a little longer. It was a long drive home and I wanted to spend as much time as I could with everyone before I went back to the real world in Cincinnati. I went to get a coffee at the vending machine with Cathy sometime after one in the morning.

She was beaming brighter than Frank. "She's just perfect!" Such a happy Grandma.

I smiled. "She is. When is Steve coming into town to meet her?"

"He's already on a flight from Rome."

"That's great. Is he happy it's a granddaughter?"

"He is, but he really wanted them to name her Stephanie."

"Why?"

"After him. Stefano."

I laughed. "Maybe the next one."

She laughed to. "When are you and Keith going to start?"

"Start what?"

"A family!"

We were headed back to the elevator to go to the waiting room. "I've told you before. I won't be a mother."

"But why not? Your kids could play with their kids and I can babysit them all!"

"We don't live near enough to each other for that."

"Small details." The elevator doors closed behind us. "What's the real reason you won't have kids. I saw the look on your face when you held that baby."

"It just wouldn't be responsible of me."

"How?"

"I have some genetic issues that would be irresponsible for me to pass on to another generation." Thanks for an out, Mom!

"Adopt."

"Do you really see Keith as a reliable father figure?"

She took a sip of her coffee as the elevator doors opened again. "I had a feeling he had something to do with it."

We were walking down a long, white corridor. "Is that bad?"

"No. Just sad."

Congratulations, Megan: By Ian

I was really proud of Megan when she graduated. Jealous. But proud. Seeing her walk across the stage of Fifth Third Arena in spring of 2013 made me a little envious, I won't lie. She was younger, had started school later, and had finished earlier than me. I felt kind of like I would never finish school and it really depressed me. I feel petty saying it out loud but at that point I had been in school for nine years.

Before her big night, I was studying at home and got a text message from her.

"You promise you will be there for me?" I could hear her angst through the text.

"Of course I will."

"Good. Dad still hasn't said if he's going or not and I already got him the ticket". Her dad was a piece of work.

"He can do what he wants but I will definitely be there for you." I tried to be reassuring. I wasn't happy about missing my night class but it was for her.

"Thanks."

I tried to cheer her up a little. *"What would you like to do to celebrate? Bonfire like we did for Frank and Suz?"*

"I think I'm still hungover from that one. LOL. Can we do something just us?"

Just us? I usually liked just us stuff. *"What did you have in mind?"*

"Take me hiking."

What the fuck? *"Why?"*

"I've never been and it's something you like to do so I want to try it."

I really did not like the sound of this but I really couldn't tell her 'no' either. *"Okay. We'll find a good trail for you."*

"YAY!"

I was really hoping she would change her mind or forget but her graduation came and went and she reminded me almost every day that she could be available whenever I was. I really didn't want to take her. It is probably going to make me sound like an asshole but I just didn't want her talking the whole time and ruining it. Hiking was my release and taking her didn't sound like a good way to decompress. And, not that she was in bad shape, she wasn't conditioned for it and I was afraid she wouldn't be able to keep up. I was right.

I'd picked her up in the morning. She was excited and showed me the new boots she had just bought for the day. I knew her feet were going to be killing her but I didn't say anything. Never break in brand new boots on a full day hike. She was smiling all through breakfast and I tried to convince myself that this wasn't going to be a bad day.   We had ended up settling on John Bryan State Park. It wasn't too rugged or too far a drive. I figured she could probably handle it. Of course it ended up being ninety-four degrees that day.

She started off fine but as it heated up, things changed pretty quickly. She needed to sit about every twenty minutes. She needed more water. Her feet were bothering her. The mosquitoes were eating her legs. She was hungry.

We stopped for snacks near the stream. I saw a boulder near the water and it immediately looked familiar. I took out my phone and snapped a picture and sent it to Suzanne.

"One of my favorite places." She wrote back.

That boulder and view of the stream was one of the paintings on her wall. I had tuned out Megan's whining and enjoyed the scenery. I could understand why she loved it here. It was away from one the more trafficked paths. There were birds and dragonflies in the water. It was shaded but still bright. Yeah. I liked this spot too.

Then reality set in and I heard Megan. "Hey. You in there?"

I turned to face her. "Sorry. Enjoying the view. What did you say?"

"I said, 'can we get a picture of the two of us here?' It's so pretty."

"Of course." I sat down next to her on the boulder and she snapped a selfie.

I looked at the picture. Here face was almost as red as her hair from the heat. Her bangs were wet and sticking to her face.

Marie Joseph-Charles 153

She looked a bit like she might heat stroke at any minute. I decided we had better keep the rest of the trip short.

When we got back to the car, she sprawled out in the passenger seat and cranked up the air conditioning.

"You okay?" She looked a little sick.

"I feel great." That was an obvious lie. "I can see why you and Suz like to do this." Another lie.

I thought about Suzanne and kind of wished she had been with me instead. "Let's get you home and hydrated." I put the car in reverse and backed out of the spot.

"And showered! I smell."

I kind of laughed. I wasn't going to tell her that.

Two Days Off: By Suzanne

I was having a rough time. Working constantly and my best friend being so far away had left me in a perpetual state of loneliness. What do the "experts" say to do when you are lonely? Stay busy! So I pick up more shifts and keep working. I'd try to keep up with everyone as best I could but my friends have lives of their own. I felt as if I had blinked and suddenly everyone was gone. My husband? I found myself less inclined to seek his company. He would get upset if I didn't want to do what he wanted; if I didn't want to see the movie he wanted or eat at the restaurant that he picked, he would get angry and frustrated. It became easier to simply avoid him. I know what you're thinking. Couples need to compromise. I believe I would have been far more likely to do so if he had ever shut up and done something I liked. Maybe let me choose the movie?   Or how about a day in the woods? No. That couldn't happen. His health was failing too much even though he wouldn't admit it for him to go for a hike. I'd consider asking him to join me but think of all the times he had and did nothing but complain that it was too hot, his calves hurt, he ran out of water… Then I'd picture him collapsing inn the middle of nowhere. He was too big for me to fireman carry to help. Part of me wasn't entirely sure I wouldn't just leave his ass there. I'm sorry. That's mean. True. But mean.

Anyways. The office manager at the clinic had a royal fit when she figured out I was working almost eighty hours a week and told me I *had* to take at least two days off in a row or she was going to force me on an unpaid sabbatical. I wasn't entirely sure it was an idle threat and so I took a Monday and Tuesday off.

Monday I set to work deep cleaning the house. I soap-and-water washed the walls. I steamed the carpets and scrubbed the tile. I set to work making a proper beef stew for dinner that was ready just in time for Keith to come home. Any minute down… Nope. He was late. He didn't even bother to tell me. The potatoes all but dissolved in the broth and the broccoli turned an unfortunately unappetizing color.

He came in and tracked dirt all over my freshly cleaned floor, dumped his collection of change, wrappers, cigarettes, etc, on the side table I had just dusted, and wrinkled his nose at he dinner I had just made.

"They bought us pizza at work so I'm not really hungry." I think the disappointment and agitation on my face were almost audible. "But that was a while ago so I'll go head and have a bowl."

I ate my soggy strew while he picked at his as we watched reruns. I hated eating in front of the TV. We had a perfectly good kitchen table where we could possibly sit and talk about our day. No.

I cleaned up the kitchen and went to bed early. I was too tired and too frustrated.

The next morning I jolted awake at 5a.m. No alarm. No cat pawing at my face. I was just awake. I had woken up my customary three to six times through the night but this time I knew there would be no falling back asleep. I looked over at Keith. He was sprawled out in all directions and snoring despite his CPAP. I rolled my eyes, rolled out of bed, and stumbled in to the kitchen with Ariel following me quickly.

With coffee made and cat fed, I sat at the table and contemplated my day. Normally with my shifts swinging from days to nights and back again, I didn't have time to really do anything. There was yard work that needed doing but it had been raining so much that everything out there was a soggy mess. Still, the thought of going outside was extremely alluring.

I poured myself more coffee and retrieved my laptop. I typed "Hiking outside of Cincinnati" into the search bar. I had hiked pretty much everything good within a two hour radius so I broadened my area. That's when I saw it. Kanawha State Park was only three and a half hours away. Even more important- it was in West Virginia. A completely different state! I looked at the clock on the stove. 5:32a.m. I could be there by 9:30. I checked the weather in Charleston. Fifty degrees and partly sunny. That settles it.

I marched back into the bedroom. I threw on some crummy jeans and a sweatshirt and dug my hiking boots out of the closet. Keith was still out cold. It would be a few more hours before he got up for work. I thought about kissing him goodbye like I used to but shook my head and closed the bedroom door behind me. I poured the remainder of the pot of coffee into a travel mug and filled a bottle full of water. I popped my meds before climbing in the car and hitting the road.

The drive was dark and peaceful. Most of the trip was rural so there were no city lights or billboards. The further away from civilization I got, the bigger the funny feeling in my gut grew. Initially, I thought it was the beginning of an anxiety attack. No two attacks are exactly the same and the damn things liked to hit me out of nowhere. The more I focused on the feeling, the more I realized it was excitement. I was just looking foreword to a day completely away from my life. I hadn't felt like this since Clifty Falls with Ian. How sad is that? I couldn't tell the difference between anxiety and happiness.

It was light by the time I reached the park. I parked at the north end towards the top of a ridge. I clipped my water bottle to my waist and set out.

It was January in 2014 so it was technically winter even though it was so warm. The trees were bare and the sky was low. I headed down into the valley first. The air was clean and the only sounds were my footsteps in the leaves and the running water in the stream. About two miles in, the trail was washed out and I had to double back. Going *down* into the valley was easy; going back *up* to get back out was hard. I hadn't noticed how steep the incline was or how much loose rock until I was willing myself every step until I made it to the top. My legs were burning and I was out of breath, but it felt great!

I managed to follow another path along the ridgeline for about a mile and a half before I decided I needed to stop for a moment. As I sat on a log, to the side of the path, I listened to the world; but I only heard my own heartbeat. There were no birds or rodents in the trees. There were no insects in the ground. There wasn't even a breeze in the branches. There was nothing. The hills and trees were brown and grey. Even the sky was colorless and quiet. There was a beauty in that that I couldn't put my finger on. I found myself wishing Ian was there with me. He was the only other person I knew who could appreciate it. I felt that familiar lonely feeling creeping through my chest and towards my throat. I swallowed it down and pressed on deeper into the woods

After about eleven miles, my legs were screaming and my muscles were threatening to mutiny. Time to go home.

The ride home wasn't nearly as quick as the drive out there. It felt as if it was taking an eternity. I think it was because I knew I didn't want to go home. That inward feeling of dread that I refused to acknowledge was making the trip drag on.

I'm not sure what time I pulled into the driveway. It was dark but it wasn't too long past supper time. When I opened the door, Keith was red and waiting for me.

"Where did you go?!" He was trying not to scream at me.

I closed the door behind me. "Hiking."

"That's not what I asked." His voice was rising.

"Kanawha." What was his problem?

"West Virginia! You went to fucking West Virginia and didn't tell me!" There's the screaming.

"Well you obviously know." I was trying to stand my ground.

"You left it up on your computer. Who went with you?"

"No one."

"So you went into the middle of nowhere in another fucking state and didn't tell anyone."

Uh-oh. "Yes." Was all I could manage.

"What the fuck were you thinking?" He swung his arm and his can of soda went flying into the wall. "You could have gotten hurt or kidnapped or died in a car crash in the mountains and no one would have known where you were!"

I suddenly felt horribly guilty and, I admit, a little scared that he was throwing things. I started sobbing. "I'm sorry." I sat on the couch with my head in my hands.

He knelt down next to me and put his hand on my shoulder. His voice softened. "Hun. I get that you needed to get away. You've been working a lot. But you've got to think before you do something so stupid. I don't want to lose you just because you decided to do something selfish."

I kept crying. "I'm so sorry."

He kissed the top of my head. "I forgive you but I'm going to go cool off in the garage for a bit."

He left me as a sobbing, guilty mess on the couch. I'm not sure how much time had passed before it hit me. Just a sec. What was he doing on my computer? I made a mental note to change the password.

Going for a Walk: Suzanne

I had officially declared myself exhausted. Fourteen hours on my feet had done me in and I was ready for dinner and a soft, comfy bed. After a shower and food, I settled into my favorite chair with a cup of chamomile tea and breathed deep. Keith was watching some football nonsense on TV that I had no interest in. I didn't care, though. All I cared about was the bed in the other room that was calling my name.

There was a knock at the door. Keith and I looked at each other. Who would be coming this late? He got up and opened it and Ian stepped in.

"What's up?" He was smiling but something was off.

I'm not an empath or anything like that, but I know the people I care about. His posture was different and, even though he was smiling, his expression wasn't genuine.

I looked him in the eye. "What's wrong?"

"Nothing. Just wanted to see what you all were up to."

"Don't lie to me. You are not okay." I was sitting up straight in my chair and looking him in the eye.

It looked like tears were trying to fight their way into his eyes. "How could you possibly tell that?"

"I'm psychic. Come on." I stood up and started to wiggle my feet into my flip-flops that were by the chair.

Keith looked confused. "Where are you going?"

"Ian and I are going for a walk."

Ian looked at me. "We are?"

"Yes. And I'm taking my tea."

My feet were swollen and my muscles ached, but Ian needed a sympathetic ear and I knew Keith didn't have one. We stepped out into the cool May night air. I was limping a little, but it was nothing I couldn't manage.

"We don't have to go anywhere." He sounded concerned.

"Yes we do. Keith is useless when it comes to this kind of thing. Bless his heart for trying but he always tries to offer advise when it is neither needed nor wanted."

"And you?"

"I'm just a vessel into which you can pour your woes."

Marie Joseph-Charles 160

"You've been reading too much."

I smiled. "Shut up and tell me what's wrong."

"It's mom. The doctors are talking hospice."

"What? I thought they got the breast cancer and she was doing well."

"They did and she was. What I didn't know is that she wasn't taking some prescription she was supposed to and it is now in her lungs and bone and she has a mass at the base of her spine. They said there's nothing they can do at this point."

"I'm so sorry, Love."

"The worst part is, I'm angry. And I feel guilty for being angry. All she needed was medicine to keep this from happening. No. She didn't do it."

"Did she tell you why?"

"She said she was tired of fighting and being in pain and the drugs were too expensive. I told her nothing was too expensive to save her life. She said she knew I would spend my school money on her and she couldn't allow it. What gives her the right to make that decision?"

"It's her life."

"She's my mother. Did she think about me and- to a lesser extent- Karen?"

"Sounds like you were the one thing she was thinking about."

"Her life is more important than school."

"Love, she *is* your mother. She wants you to live your life. That's why she gave it to you and has done everything she could for you up to this point. She doesn't want to hold you back or slow you down any more than she has over the last few years."

"And that's where it becomes my life and she doesn't have the right to decide that for me."

"And you have the right to force her to live when she is ready to let go?"

He stopped walking and turned to face me. He opened his mouth to say something and then closed it. He looked at the sky and turned his back to me.

I walked up and put my hand on his shoulder. "How long does she have?"

"Couple months. Maybe."

"Then make it worth it while you can."

He turned and hugged me. We rounded the cul-de-sac at the end of the street and headed back to my house in silence. We parted ways in the driveway and I went into the house to explain things to Keith. He was pretty shaken. Ian's mom had been family to him too since they were kids.

About a month and a half later, I was again having tea in my favorite chair. Keith wasn't home and it was a peaceful evening with Ariel. There was a knock at the door. I opened it. Ian was in a state I had never seen. He looked at me and fell to his knees. He wrapped his arms around my legs and sobbed. I kneeled down on the ground with his head in my lap. His tears soaked through my sweatpants but his sobs broke my heart. He was in pain. True pain. And there was nothing I could do. I just held his head and let him cry.

Goodbye, Mom: by Ian

My mother's death was the hardest thing I had ever been through. I don't wish hospice on anyone. I had to sit there and watch what was left of the woman who gave me everything literally just waste away. She only weighed fifty-something pounds in the end. It wasn't long before she couldn't hear me tell her I love her. She couldn't feel me holding her hand. She couldn't see me crying next to her. Day after day we sat and just waited for her to die. My sister and Brent moved in with their brats so she could "help" even though I told her the hospice nurse had everything under control. She insisted as if I didn't know she was looking for a copy of the will or snooping through mom's jewelry while I was gone. One of the last lucid things my mother had said to me was to ask for a promise to continue going to school. While I seriously hated the idea of leaving my sister alone with her, I kept my promise and went to school up until the day she was officially comatose.

After the coma, we stayed in the living room as a "family." Every time she opened her mouth to gasp for air, I thought, *This is it. She's gone.* But the heart monitor kept beeping for a few days.

I had dozed off in the chair next to the hospital bed the hospice people had brought into the living room for her. I hadn't been sleeping well between dealing with my idiot sister, her family, school, and worry about Mom. Karen and Brent were sleeping in Mom's bed (believe me, I fought that one) and their kids were in Karen's old room. Megan had fallen asleep on the couch. She had insisted on staying with me every night after Mom went into the coma. She really was a great girlfriend.

It woke me up from a stone sleep. It was a little after eleven at night on July 8th of '14. The heart monitor had changed from a beeping noise to one long, loud tone. I grabbed Mom's hand and shook it. I knew she wouldn't wake up from the coma but I knew that sound was worse than a coma. The hospice nurse put her stethoscope on Mom's chest. She kind of checked a few places and then took it out of her ears and nodded at me.

That was it. The woman who had given me everything was gone.

Marie Joseph-Charles 164

Megan came up and wrapped her arms around my neck. I leaned into her arm a little but I didn't let go of Mom's arm or turn my head.

She kissed my head. "I'll go wake up Karen." She squeezed me and went upstairs.

Karen was the last person I wanted to deal with but I was just kind of numb. I wasn't crying. I wasn't angry. We'd known this was coming for almost two months so I should have resolved any feelings about it. I should have been perfectly ready to accept this. But I wasn't. I didn't know how to feel so I just went numb.

Karen came running down the stairs. She was exaggerated sobbing and threw herself at Mom's body. The kids' tears were real. Grandma Gloria was gone. Brent was kneeling on the floor and trying to comfort his kids while his wife put on the performance of a lifetime.

I was still holding Mom's arm when Megan came up behind me again. She put her hand on my shoulder. This time I stood and turned up faced her. I was done watching my sister's bullshit acting.

"I'm going to go so you can have time with your family."

I grabbed her hands. "I love you."

She looked startled. Looking back on it, I realize that the first time I had ever told her I loved her, in all the years that we were together, was standing next to my mother's dead body.

She stood on her toes and kissed my cheek. "I'll call and check on you tomorrow." She squeezed my hands and left.

I turned back to everyone. Karen was wiping her fake tears with a paper towel. "Who's the executor of her will?"

"Seriously? You're going straight to her will?" I suddenly felt something. Hatred. He was a familiar friend when my sister was involved.

"Calm down. We need to know if she specified a funeral home or what she wants us to do with her body."

"Uncle Pete's the executor. If you were ever around to talk to her about it, you would know she's being cremated by Oak and Anders because she didn't want everyone's last memory of her to be like this." I held my arm out to mom.

The hospice nurse quietly backed out and into the den. Brent took the kids back upstairs.

"I'm sorry I have a family to take care of and couldn't be here every day."

"Fuck your bullshit, Karen! You live ten minutes away!"

"Maybe I didn't want to watch her waste away. Did you ever think of that?"

"Oh, get over yourself! You didn't want to watch Mom get sick so you just left her to me? Really? Do you realize how fucking selfish that sounds? What's your excuse for before she got sick?"

"That's your play? The 'pity-me' card? It didn't work when you were little either. How would mom have felt dying and knowing that you thought she was such a burden on you?"

I snapped. I grabbed the rocking chair the hospice nurse had been sitting in and threw it into the wall with one arm. I think I heard myself roar when I did it. Karen backed up. She knew she'd gone too far. I knew I had to leave. NOW. As I went out the front door, I ripped the key hook out of the wall when I grabbed my car keys and I slammed the front door hard enough that the house shook. I didn't care. If I didn't leave right then, I didn't know what I was going to do.

I started driving. I couldn't focus. I couldn't think. Nothing felt real. There was no road. There were no other cars or traffic signals. The only thing that was real was my hatred for Karen.

I didn't know where I was going until I got there. The red door didn't feel real when I knocked on it. Nothing felt real until she opened the door. When I saw Suzanne, everything hit me at once and I just fucking crumbled. I was just sobbing and shaking into her knees and holding her. I couldn't let go of her. She felt real. She kind of put her arms around my head and rocked me a little. I have no idea how long we were like that but I know it was at least an hour.

She helped me up and took me inside and the next thing I knew, it was morning. Apparently, she had laid me on the couch and went to make me something to drink but I had passed out by the time she came back. Now, she was sitting on the edge of the

foot stool with a mug of coffee and gently scratching the back of
my shoulder and telling me to wake up.

I tried to open my eyes but they were swollen from crying.
She helped me hold the coffee. "Drink this. It'll help."
I sat up slowly. My whole body hurt. "What time is it?"
"A bit after nine. Keith already left for work but he wanted
me to tell you that he will call you later. I was going to let you
sleep but I wasn't sure if you needed to go home and take care of
your mom." She sat in her favorite chair near me with her own cup
of coffee.

Last night's blur was starting to come back to me. My
mom was dead and I had wanted to kill my sister.

"How many of those have you had?" I pointed at her
coffee.

"This one makes three. I've been up for a while."
"Do you sleep?"
"Not as long as I have this." She smiled and drank more
coffee.

I looked at my mug. "I don't want to go home."
"I know, Love. But you need to. You know you are
welcome here and we can make up the spare bed for you. But you
need to go take care of your family."

"What family? My mom is gone and my sister is a piece of
shit who can go to Hell."

"What about your aunts, uncles, and cousins? Won't they
want to know?"

I took a deep breath. "Yeah. I guess so."

I finished my coffee and went home. I've never wanted to
avoid something so much in my life. When I pulled into the
driveway, I saw what was left of the rocking chair in pieces next to
the garbage by the side of the house. When I went inside, Karen
was sitting in the living room with Uncle Pete. The hospice people
had already come and taken the bed and everything was back
where it belonged. Pete and I looked at each other, we both
nodded, and I went upstairs to get a shower.

When I came back down, Pete motioned for me to sit.
I looked at Karen. "I'd rather stand."

"Sit. Down." Pete was an old guy but the respectful little boy that was intimidated by him when I was growing up was still there and I did as I was told. "Your mom gave me strict instructions not to read the will until after the funeral. I am to referee any disputes between you two and anyone who doesn't play by the rules gets booted out. Is this clear?"

Karen looked across the coffee table at me. "I'll behave if he does."

I scoffed.

"What did I just say?" There's the Uncle Pete I was afraid of.

"Sorry, Sir." I felt like I was six years old again.

The funeral was the following Thursday. I was glad to see how many people piled into the church to say goodbye to Mom. Karen and I stood on opposite sides of the door to thank people for coming as they walked in. I just wished they would have stopped saying "I'm sorry for your loss." "Your mom was a special lady." "You'll be okay." After about the hundredth person, it starts to lose all meaning.

When we took our seats, Megan sat to my left and squeezed my had tight. Brent sat in between me and Karen and the kids sat in the back with Aunt Leena because, let's face it, two of them were too little to understand that this wasn't a normal day at church and wouldn't hold still.

When it was my turn to stand up and speak, I completely lost my nerve. I looked around at a church full of people and had no idea what I had prepared to say. I found Suzanne in the crowd with Frank, Brian, and Keith. My sister was right. I was selfish. I had completely neglected *that* family. I hadn't called to tell any of them. Suzanne had made sure they were all there for me.

"I think I had picked a couple Bible verses to quote today but I don't think I'm going to use them. The only reason Mom wanted her funeral in a church was to make the rest of you happy." A lot of people looked kind of shocked and, I guess, annoyed by that. I kept going. "But that's because that's the kind of person she was right up even after her death. She always put her heart's wants and needs aside so that the rest of us could be happy or have our wants. Selfless sacrifice until the end. I don't think of myself as a mama's boy, but she was more than a mom. She was my best friend. She gave everything for me and Karen and we never knew we were missing out on anything. How many of you knew that after our dad left, she would go without dinner to save money? She would lie to her kids and tell us that she would eat later or that she had big lunch at work so we wouldn't know she was starving for us. She lied to her brothers and sisters so they wouldn't feel like they needed to help her or take care of her kids. She didn't want to be a burden on anyone." I shot Karen a look. "I can only hope that when I die, I have done everything I can to make her proud."

After the church service, everyone came back to the house for sandwiches and stuff that Karen had catered in. The house was busting. I had no idea so many people would come back to eat and share stories. Megan and I had somehow found a corner in the den to sit together in silence. That's where she found us.

"What you said about Mom going hungry for us. Was that true?"

It felt like the whole room had gone quiet. "Yes."

"How do you know?"

"I used to hear her crying in the kitchen. I'd sit with her until I fell asleep and she'd put me back to bed. I always heard her stomach but she never ate. I figured it out eventually."

"Why didn't she ever say anything to me about it? I'm older. I could have helped."

"Did you listen to what I said at all? She didn't want anyone worrying about her and let's face it, you were too busy doing your own thing anyway."

That was the first time I'd seen Karen cry real tears and she turned and left.

It was another week before the will was read. I understood why Mom didn't want it read before the funeral. We each went in turn. Aunts and Uncles got knickknacks and family heirlooms. But Karen! She got the house! The house that *I* grew up in! The house that *I* took care of when mom was sick. I was furious. Then it was my turn. There was a lawyer present for me. He told me to come to him when I had finished my degree. Mom had set up a fund with a hundred and twenty thousand dollars for me and me alone. I was to finish my education and the money was to pay for it. Whatever was left was mine to keep. I had no idea she had that kind of money. She really could have afforded more treatment. I guess she really was just tired of fighting. I didn't tell anyone. Karen would have contested it and I didn't want to deal with all of that. Well, I did tell one person. Suzanne swore herself to secrecy.

My New Place: By Ian

It was hard to leave my childhood home. That little house was pretty much the only thing I knew (other than when I was away for school). Karen offered to let me stay, but there was no way that was going to happen. I'd kill her and her bratty little kids in their sleep. Besides, Josh, the oldest, had already staked a claim on my room.

Megan had wanted us to get a place together. She said rent would be cheaper if we shared and it would be nice to have 'a place to call ours.' I won't say I was completely opposed to the idea. I mean, I loved her and all and financially it did make more sense, but in the end I said no. It's not that I didn't want to wake up to her every morning. I had never lived on my own. Even when I lived in Cleveland, I shared living space. This was something I felt like I had to do for myself for now. I still hadn't completely recovered from Mom's death and I didn't think I'd be a good roommate anyway. I was sure that was the nagging 'no' voice I kept hearing in my head.

Of all days, we settled on a Wednesday for the move. Getting a truck was cheaper and Keith and Megan said they could come help after work. Suzanne was off her third shift that morning and said she could come help after she'd had a little sleep. I was okay with that. She got off at eight so I expected to see her later in the afternoon. Nope. I had to pick up the rental truck at noon and she was there waiting for me.

"I thought you had to sleep."

"I did."

"Not very much, obviously."

She held up a Styrofoam cup of coffee. "We're good."

"You are going to die of sleep deprivation."

"It's a distinct possibility."

They did the initial inspection of the truck and I initialed my life away to rent it. When I was finally handed the keys, we climbed in.

Suzanne was sitting next to me in the passenger seat. "You know you're going to have to make multiple trips, right?"

"What do you mean?"

"This truck is too small."

"No. The description said 'one bedroom apartment or studio apartment.'"

"Okay… Maybe I should drive my car too so we can squeeze some stuff in it too." She got back out of the truck and went to her car.

We pulled up in front of the little, white house. I never really stopped to appreciate how pretty it was. I hated doing Mom's flower beds while she was sick, but she loved them so much and took such good care of them while she could, I couldn't let her down. Karen and her spawn were at their house. I assumed they were packing to swarm into my former home.

I let us in. A lot of the small furniture, fancy dishes, and things were gone. We had let family members who weren't included in the will request mementos of mom. Our family was pretty big so they cleaned out a lot of it. I took a deep breath and looked around.

"Do you need a minute?" Suzanne came up and put her hand on my shoulder.

"No. Let's just get this done."

"Where do you want to start?"

"The den, I guess. I'm taking the smaller couch and chairs and stuff. Karen is bringing her furniture from her house."

"Let's get to it, Love."

"The bigger stuff can wait until Keith is off or we have more help."

She rolled her eyes and picked up the end of the couch. "Are you going to get the other end or am I dragging this out to the truck?"

I couldn't help but smile at her. I should have known better than to make a comment like that.

It took a few hours but we loaded pretty much the whole living room and kitchen into the truck. We'd put little stuff like lamps in Suz's car but other than that, I was feeling pretty proud. The truck was packed but the back gate could still close.

"See!" I nudged her with my elbow. "I told you it would fit."

"Don't you have an entire bedroom to load still?"

I felt my face fall. She was right. We'd only done two rooms. I hate to think what the look on my face said, but she just laughed at me and said we'd get it on the next trip.

When I got out of the truck at the new apartment, I felt a little sick. I stood staring up. My apartment was on the third floor. We were going to have to carry all of this up three flights of stairs. And they weren't just straight up. Oh, no. These things zigzagged. Fuck.

I swear that woman could read my mind. Suzanne just walked passed me carrying a lamp. "It's called a freight elevator." And kept walking.

She was right. There was an elevator at the back of the building. We loaded it as best we could and had the truck emptied fairly quickly. I didn't really care where anything was at that point. I just wanted to get it all done. It was a small studio apartment. There was a kitchen area, a bathroom, and space for a bed and living area. It was all a guy like me needed.

There was stuff everywhere by the time we were ready to go back to get the next load. I had already packed my possessions in boxes. We took the mattress and box spring down first. My bed frame, though, was this big, heavy, awkward wooden monstrosity. As we were carrying down the stairs, her hand slipped and it fell over. It left a pretty bad hole in the wall.

"Oh, my God! I'm so sorry."

I laughed. I swung the top corner of the end I had into the other side and put another hole in it. "Oops." I smiled.

"Your sister is going to be pissed."

"What do I care?"

She smiled and looked kind of relieved that I wasn't mad at her.

We somehow managed to get the dresser, night stand, and boxes down without any more holes in the drywall. Round two. We unloaded at the apartment and flopped down on the couch against each other. It was a little after five and I think we were both tired.

I took a deep breath. Despite the hard work and sweat, she still smelled like flowers.

"Is that it?" She stretched her legs out in front of her and yawned.

"Should be. Anything else should be small enough that I can get on my own."

"Good."

I looked down at her. We hadn't been this close since Frank's wedding and it made me feel… weird. "Thank you for helping."

"What are friends for? You are feeding me, right?"

I laughed. "I think I can do that." I almost kissed the top of her head. Why would I do that? Thank God I stopped myself.

"You two look cozy." Megan was standing in the doorway.

"Exhausted is more like it." Suz sat up.

I stood and went to Megan. "Glad you could make it." I tried to kiss her but she gave me the cheek. Uh-oh.

"I got this for you." She shoved a little potted bush in my hands.

"Uh. Thanks."

She looked around. "It looks crowded."

"Still have to put things a way and figure out where everything is going to go. I thought you could help with that."

"Glad I'll be able to help with something." She sounded bitter and I thought for a second that she gave Suzanne a look.

Suz stretched again. "Pizza? I'll go get beer."

I looked at her. "You don't drink beer."

"You do. And I guarantee Keith will want something. Chardonnay good with you, Megan?"

Megan's face kind of softened. "Sounds good to me!"

Suzanne left and I turned and took Megan's hands. "I'm sorry we did all of the big stuff without you. But now you get to help me with the fun stuff."

"How, so?"

"I'm not an interior decorator. And this isn't a bachelor pad. I need your womanly touch."

She kind of smiled. "Okay. You order pizza. I'll have a look around."

Keith showed up around the same time as the pizza. We ate, drank, and horsed around. At some point, the girls were sitting with glasses of wine and pointing to tell us where to move things. Later, Megan started unboxing some stuff and calling out things like 'Japanese shoji' and 'dishes' while Suzanne wrote them down. Apparently, I had some shopping to do.

Megan had gotten the sleeping area (a corner near the windows) pretty much set up and had piled boxes labeled "clothes" at the foot of the bed. I opened one box and there was a faux leather book with my name on it on top. I smiled and looked at Suzanne. She and Megan were explaining something to Keith but he wasn't listening. I put the book on my night stand.

It was about three in the morning before we got to sleep. The four of us spent my first night in my new apartment together. Suzanne slept on the couch, Keith on the floor, and me and Megan in my bed. Megan still seemed like something was bothering her but I didn't want to push the issue.

Girl Talk: By Suzanne

There is nothing more therapeutic than two best friends, some take-out sushi, and a couple of bottles of wine! It was February of 2015. Frank's mom had been bugging for Frank to bring the babies into town (even though she had just seen them at Christmas). Frank caved. She and Brian came to Cincinnati and her mom kept them busy all day. She and Steve insisted on taking the girls out for new clothes because 'kids grow like weeds and these rags won't fit too much longer.' You have to love grandparents. Frank and Brian tagged along to keep Cathy from spending too much money. Finally, around 7 p.m., they had maxed out at least one credit card and the kids were getting fussy.

Frank and Brian left the kids with her parents. Brian and Keith went out to a bar or something while we split dinner and a bottle (or two).

"You have no idea how much I missed this!" Franked popped a slice of sushi into her mouth.

I was not so graceful with chopsticks and fiddled with my piece before I succeeded in picking it up. "Me too!"

"What have I missed?"

"Not a damn thing."

"I kind of miss the old clinic." She downed some chardonnay.

"Why? You have a day practice job. No crazy hours. No crazy emergencies…"

"Plenty of crazy clients though! Oh, my God, I have this one woman who doesn't believe in 'big pharma' antibiotics and decided that, since we couldn't give medical grade drugs, she would feed this poor poodle a BUNCH of food that she had let get moldy on purpose so it could get 'natural' antibiotics!"

"Tremorgenic mycotoxins?"

"Yup. Got the report from the Indianapolis ER on the fax machine. Dog ended up dying because she kept arguing with them about treatment."

"People are fucking crazy."

"Yup."

I managed another piece with the chop sticks. "So, what do you miss?"

"I don't know. The adrenaline rush. The people. Don't get me wrong, there are plenty of nice people where I'm at now, but it's not the same family feeling."

"You can always come home."

She kind of laughed. "I don't think I could get Brian to agree to that. But we do need to get together more often."

I suddenly kind of felt like I was going to cry. "Yeah. We do."

"Is everything okay?" She could see right into me, I swear.

"I guess so. I'm just working so many ridiculous shifts to make sure I'm getting bills and my student loans paid. Keith keeps spending all his extra money on car crap but it's his money so I can't say anything as long as bills are getting paid."

"Um. Yes. You can say something. You guys are supposed to be in this together."

"Tell him that." I pushed the sushi around a little with my chopsticks. "I don't even think he knows where the vacuum cleaner is kept. Or how to run the wash machine. He outright refuses to scrub the toilet."

"What chores does he do?"

"Sometimes he'll load the dishwasher."

"That's…. not okay, actually."

"I know. I try to talk to him about it. But, you know him."

"Gets defensive."

"And turns it around back on me." I downed the rest of my glass of wine.

She poured more into my glass and then hers. "Suz. I love you both. But you aren't happy. That's really not okay."

"I know. I think a lot of it is just that I'm so exhausted all the time."

"Then he should be helping more."

"I'm sure he does and I'm just not acknowledging it."

She kind of laughed. "I've known Keith since we were in diapers. I seriously doubt it."

"How do you and Brian make things work?"

"Truthfully," she smiled, "I took your advice. We worked things out before we moved in together. Then we reworked them when Amber was born. Then we went back and looked at things again when Christina was born. You told me that night over milkshakes to communicate with him and it's worked great."

"I'm glad you were able to learn from my mistakes."

"Seriously. You need to talk to him. Threaten to kick him out, if you have to!"

I laughed and choked a little on some wine. "I don't have to. He usually leaves on his own."

"He still does that toddler temper tantrum crap where he leaves angry?"

"Yup. And comes back and acts like nothing ever happened."

"Oh, my God. He's been doing that since he was little! I wonder if he's grown up at all."

"I didn't know him when he was a kid, but I doubt it. It's like a clothes hamper doesn't even exist!"

"Oh, that's just a guy thing! Does he leave dirty things hanging on the bathroom doorknob?"

"Ew. No. But he leaves dirty clothes EVERYWHERE!"

We both laughed. We ate a few more pieces of sushi. The whole air suddenly became very solemn.

"Suz…"

"I know." She didn't even have to say it.

The front door suddenly flung open and Brian and Keith came in loudly. Keith was very clearly drunk.

"You guys weren't gone very long." Frank sounded disappointed.

"Keith picked a fight with a guy at the bar so I figured we had better leave." Brian helped Keith sit in his recliner.

"I did not pick a fight! That fucker started it! He called me a fat ass." Keith's nose was red. He'd had A LOT to drink.

Brian ignored him. "I'm sorry. I thought we could just hang out here and watch some TV."

Frank looked at me and smiled. "You thinking what I'm thinking?"

I smiled back at her. "Yup. I'll get the sushi. You get the wine."

"Where are you going?" Brian looked confused.

"There is a perfectly good bedroom in the back with a queen-sized bed."

"You aren't going to watch TV with us?" Keith sounded annoyed. I didn't care.

"No. We're going to have a little girl talk."

We went into my room and shut the door. We spread out on the bed with wine on the night stands.

"Remember studying like this?" Frank was grinning wide.

"I remember having too much wine and forgetting what we were studying."

"Exactly! I miss that."

"Me too." I flicked a little piece of salmon on the floor. Ariel had been watching us intently in the kitchen and followed us into the bedroom. He deserved something out of all of this.

"You need to get out hiking more."

"I know." She was right. "I can always clear my head and relax when I've been in the woods for a while."

"Maybe Keith could go with you. Have a date."

I looked at her. "You're joking, right?"

She smiled. "Kind of. You two do need a date."

"We went to Cavalcade last year."

"*Last year.* And that's not a date. You don't like cars."

"And he's going to go to a museum with me?"

"Maybe not. Dinner and a movie?"

"We do dinner all the time. And he doesn't like going to movie theaters because he swears he's going to get bedbugs or lice."

"Jeez. He's really gotten high maintenance."

I laughed. "Tell me about it! What do you and Brian do for dates?"

"We take turns. I'll go to a football game for him and he'll go to chick flick with me. Stuff like that. We do each other's things."

"That sounds reasonable."

"What did you and Keith used to do? When you were more happy?"

I thought about it. "I… I honestly can't remember."

"Do you even remember being happy?"

"I think so. But I don't remember what it was that made me happy."

"You should think about it. Find that happy thing again."

"You make it sound like I haven't tried." We had switched to white zinfandel and I swished the wine in circles in my glass.

"I'm sorry. You know what I mean, though."

"I know. Can we switch topics now?"

She smiled big and sat up straight. "Guess what Amber did while we were out?"

Okay. We can talk about the kids. That's, at least, not talking about me. "What?"

"She told my mom 'no' when mom tried to put a bonnet on her!"

"Smart kid!"

"Oh, I know! She's going to be a problem child with her attitude and intelligence."

"Sounds like she's her mother's daughter."

"That is EXACTLY what Brian said!"

We drank and talked about the kids for a few more hours. It was getting late and we were all tired. Brian took Frank home. I looked at Keith. He was passed out in his chair. I had no desire to wake him. He snored loudly. I thought about bringing out his CPAP and putting it on him for the night but decided against it. It was more trouble than it was worth.

I changed into my pajamas and sprawled out in the bed. I had the whole thing to myself! Well, Ariel and I had the whole thing. It was nice. I was feeling relaxed partly from so much wine (we really did have A LOT of wine) and partly because I had finally had time with my best friend. I really missed that.

She was Crying: by Ian

It was April in '15. I was supposed to go over to help
Keith with his car (not the Corvair). He said the transmission was
sluggish or something like that. I really didn't pay much attention
when he asked me for help. It was an excuse to get out of the
apartment that wasn't school or work; not that Megan wasn't a
good distraction. When I pulled in front of their house, I didn't see
his car in the driveway. I knew it wasn't in the garage because
there were the pieces of the Corvair and more tools and tool chests
than he could ever use. I shrugged it off and knocked on the door.
I knew Suzanne would yell at me for knocking; she always said
that I'm family and can come in any time. I prepared myself for a
stern talking-to but nothing prepared me for what I saw when the
door opened.

Suzanne's eyes were red and swollen. Her face was damp
and her hair was a mess. She'd been crying. Not like normal
woman hormonal crying at the cute puppy on TV. No. She had
been seriously crying.

I should have hugged her. Instead I kind of gaped at her at
her. "Jesus Christ. What the Hell happened?"

Ever say exactly the WRONG thing? Yeah. That was it. I
knew that was it before I even finished saying it. Halfway through
the sentence and for some reason I didn't shut up and say
something else. Her jaw started to shake and her eyes filled again.

"Oh, God. I'm sorry. Fuck. I'm sorry. I meant 'are you
okay?'" Too late. Damage done. I'm a jerk.

She sat in her rocking chair and I sat on the couch near her.

She took a deep breath and wiped her eyes. "Keith and I
got into a pretty big fight."

"Where is he now?"

"Went for a drive. He'll be back in a little bit and act like
nothing happened. He always does."

"What *did* happen?"

She took another deep breath. Ariel jumped in her lap and
she started petting him. "Yesterday, he locked his keys in the car
and I have the spare. I was at work. I don't keep my phone on me
at work. He had called and texted a bunch of times, but I didn't

get any of the messages until I got off. I messaged him back and told him I was on my way. By that point it was rush hour and raining. When I finally got home, he was soaking wet and pissed. I let him in the house to change and got his keys out of his car. He was so mad. He didn't talk to me at all after that. Then today I asked him about you coming over and he just exploded. I guess he just kept everything bottled up from last night. He said I'm selfish and vindictive and that I made him sit in the rain for two hours on purpose because I was punishing him for something. He said I'm cruel and that he's tired of me taking everything out on him. When I asked him what he was talking about he started screaming a whole bunch of stuff about how I'm always punishing him when he didn't do anything wrong and that I never want to spend time with him any more and… I don't know. He was really yelling a lot of things." Another tear fell out of her right eye.

When I get angry, I feel like my body temperature instantly rises. It's kind of like that whole saying that 'your blood is boiling.' When I saw her shed a tear because of Keith, my blood instantly hit close to two hundred Kelvin. I tried not to show her I was angry. I didn't want her to think I was angry *at her*. "Here's my question: Doesn't your dad live like fifteen minutes away and have a spare house key?"

"Yeah."

"Why didn't he call him and have him unlock the door?"

"I wish you could answer that."

"And if he doesn't know what you're punishing him for, why does he think you are punishing him at all?"

"Fuck if I know."

"And aren't you working like sixty hours a week right now?"

"Yes."

"So, he thinks you're working to avoid spending time with him?"

"I guess."

"None of that makes any sense."

"I know. I really don't know what just happened."

Perfect timing. Keith walked in with a grocery bag. He smiled. "Hey man! Glad you could make it. Stupid car is just not right. I knew I shouldn't have bought German." He faced Suz as he walked in the kitchen. "Hun, I got chicken for dinner and those little potato things you like."

Suzanne swallowed hard. "Okay."

She was right. Here she was a total wreck and he walked in as if nothing at all had happened. Now, I'm not a relationship expert but I'm pretty sure something like that is not okay.

He set the grocery bag in the refrigerator and headed to the garage door. "I'm going to open the garage and start getting out tools. See you out there in a minute?"

I was kind of stunned for a second. "Uh. Yeah."

"Cool." He closed the door behind him.

I turned to Suzanne. "Is he always like that after a fight?"

"Yeah. And the bigger the fight, the more he acts like nothing happened. It's better than little fights. He holds grudges for days and it's always my fault."

"That's not normal or healthy." She looked down at her cat. I'm not sure if she was embarrassed or ashamed. "Are you going to be okay?"

"I always am. Are you staying for dinner? Apparently, we are having chicken and potatoes."

"Would that be wise? I don't want to get in the way of you two talking more."

"First of all, there is no talking; only yelling. Second, he won't bring it up again until his next explosion-"

"Wait, how often does this happen?"

"Increasing frequency." She continued without hesitating. "Third, I'd really like your company right now."

She looked through my eyes and into a part of my heart that hurt for her. "Okay."

She squeezed my hand. "Thank you, Love. You'd better get out there before he finds something else to yell about."

I squeezed her hand back and stood up. I walked out the front door and Keith already had his hood up.

He looked at me with an oil rag in his hand. "I changed the fluids last weekend and that didn't do the trick. I think either the disk is bad or it could be the gear teeth are worn. Maybe a solenoid problem."

I swallowed down some of my anger (kind of how Suzanne was a few minutes ago). "What's it doing?"

"Grinding. Not wanting to change gears."

I looked into the engine bay. "Look man, I don't know if it's my place to say anything." I looked over at him.

He looked instantly irritated. "Then don't."

"Suzanne is my friend."

"And I'm not? Besides, she's my WIFE."

"I just want to look out for both of you."

"Then stay out of it."

"Look, Dude. I meant what I said at your wedding."

"I get it. I shouldn't have blown up at her. It is what it is. We'll move on like we always do."

"Are you going to apologize or anything?"

"I did. I bought her potatoes."

"What the fuck? Since when is buying a woman potatoes an apology?"

"I did something nice for her. That's the same as saying 'I'm sorry.'"

"No. No, I'm pretty sure it's not. You're supposed to do nice things for your wife without having a reason. The fact that it's automatically an apology in your book is kind of fucked up."

"Trust me. When you're married and all that lovey-dovey honeymoon phase is worn off, you'll get it."

I was left seriously dumbfounded. No, I wasn't married but I felt like I had a better grasp of how marriage worked than Keith did. I looked at the window of the house. Suzanne was looking back at me. She shook her head and held her fingers to her lips in a 'shhhh' motion. Okay. I would drop it. For now at least. But only because she asked me to.

We dicked around in the car for a couple of hours. I don't remember what exactly was wrong with it but it was something he couldn't fix that day. I do remember Suzanne opening the front door and calling us to dinner.

The table was set for three. There was pop already poured for us and a glass of wine for her. I guess she needed it after that fight. I knew she wasn't supposed to be mixing alcohol with her meds but I trusted she knew her limit and didn't say anything. On the stove was a cast iron skilled full of chicken and potatoes. The thing that struck me as total bullshit was that she had to cook her own apology potatoes.

Nerve Damage: By Suzanne

This all happened in late summer or early fall of 2016. It was around six in the morning on a Sunday. My Saturday overnight shift was not yet over but there was a light at the end of the tunnel. LeeAnn, one of my best technicians, escorted a limping Chesapeake Bay retriever into the treatment area. If you have never seen one, picture a brown, one hundred pound, curly haired Labrador but without the sweet and goofy disposition.

I was entering notes from another patient into the computer while she and an assistant collected vital signs. The dog seemed calm and comfortable throughout the process. When she was satisfied, she brought me his patient chart.

She set it in my hand. "TPR is within normal limits. Owners said they let him out for his morning pee and he came back in limping. No blood or visible trauma."

"Okay. He'll probably need radiographs. Charity," I looked over at the assistant, "can you get the x-ray machine prepped?"

I took the chart over to the dog. He wagged his tail but his body language was cautionary. LeeAnn put an arm around his neck to control his head and one around his body. He was a large dog and she was a not-so-large person, but everything seemed okay. I looked in his eyes, ears, mouth, and at his skin. Good so far. But that's when it happened. I picked up his front leg to examine the foot. Without warning, he slipped his head out of LeeAnn's grasp and latched onto my forearm. I remember him shaking his head in attempt to separate my meat from the bone. I don't remember how they got him to let go but I remember one of the girls frantically wrapping my arm in a towel.

The upside of a dog bite is that it is more of a crushing injury than a puncture when compared to a cat bite. This meant that there was very little blood. The down side is that there is more potential for tissue bruising and nerve damage and his attempt to alligator the muscle off my arm had only caused further impairment. I was going to need to go to the hospital. I hate human hospitals.

Marie Joseph-Charles 187

I calmly asked the receptionist to call Dr. Stone to come in and replaced me. I told LeeAnn to take a walk and calm down. She was sobbing and blaming herself for getting me bit. I then asked my assistant to call Keith to meet me at the hospital.

En route to the hospital, I tried to call Keith myself. Twenty-two times. In the seventeen minutes between when I left work and pulled into the parking lot at the hospital, the girls and I had tried to call him a combined twenty-two times. None of us got an answer. There was no doubt in my mind that he was peacefully adrift in dreamland. That man could sleep through anything.

I pulled into a parking space and shut off my car. It was my right arm that was damaged and I was devoutly right handed. I called the only person I was sure would come to help me.

"Yeah?" Ian sounded groggy and irritable.

"I'm sorry to wake you, Love. I'm at the ER. I got attacked by a dog and my right arm is pretty mangled up. Can you meet me and help me with the paperwork and stuff?" Halfway through talking I could hear bedsprings and rustling in the background.

"Where are you?" He sounded a little distant like he had se the phone down.

"Mercy."

"On my way."

I walked in the emergency room and explained what happened and that I had a scribe on the way. They took me straight back to a curtained exam area. They asked a lot of questions about the animal's vaccination status and workman's comp. It was standard bite protocol stuff. One of the ladies brought be an ice pack to help with the swelling. I swear that whole bit took less than ten minutes when Ian came bursting through the curtain.

"Are you okay?" His eyes were wide.

He was wearing pajama bottoms, a hoodie that was a bit too small and might have been Megan's, mismatched socks, and flip flops. He had obviously quite literally thrown on the first clothes he grabbed. He lived a good fifteen minutes away from that hospital and I had woken him up when I called. Just how many speed limits had he broken?

"I'm fine, Love." I tried to sound reassuring. "Can you fill out paperwork for me? You may need to call the office to get the workman's comp info."

"Of course! I'll be right back." He allowed one of the ladies to take him back to the front desk.

After a battery of further questioning, radiographs, and an MRI of my arm, they said they were going to have to sedate me for some other thing I don't remember. Ian stayed with me through all of it and promised he would be there when I woke up.
While I was out, he tried to call Keith a few more times but without luck. When I came to, my right arm was bandaged. On my left, Ian was in a chair with his head resting on the bed near my arm. I reached out and touched his hair. He kind of yawned and stretched. I think he had been dozing off.

"How do you feel?" He looked me in the eye and took my hand. There was so much concern in those yes.

"Yeah. I feel fine. A little sore. What time is it?"

"Going on ten."

"Shouldn't you be at work right now?"

"I called them and explained that I had somewhere important to be at the moment and I'd come in later."

I smiled at him. He didn't have to do that for me. "Thank you, Love."

Before he could say anything, I caught a familiar whiff of cigarette smell just as Keith pulled back the curtain. "I slept through my phone."

He was fully dressed and had an energy drink in his hand. At least he wasn't so concerned about me that he couldn't stop by the gas station on the way.

"I figured." I let go of Ian's hand and pushed myself more upright in the bed.

Keith shot a look at Ian just as a nurse shoved passed him. "All ready to go over your discharge instructions?"

Ian looked back at Keith. "See, dude. You're just in time." He turned to me. "I'm going to go ahead into work. I'll check in on you later." He squeezed my good hand.

I looked back at those brown eyes. "Thank you, again."

"Glad I could be here for you." He met Keith's gaze before pushing passed him. I think he was really pissed at my husband for not being there for me.

I was discharged with instructions to rest it, ice it, and take plenty of anti-inflammatory drugs. I got lucky. There was no serious nerve damage as far as they could tell. There was quite a bit of muscle damage and I was warned to take it easy for several weeks. Great.

Keith and I drove home separately. I kind of wanted to stay in the safety and quiet of the hospital. After the look he shot Ian, I knew I was going to get an earful when we got home. I was right. No sooner had we walked in the front door than Keith started.

"You called Ian! Why?"

I closed the door behind me. "Frank is two hours away."

"Don't be cute. You could have told him to come over and wake me up."

"Why would I think to do that? I was in pain. I just needed someone to come to help me."

"*I'm* your husband."

"No shit!" I was mad and still feeling a bit drugged but it surprised me how easily that flew out of my mouth.

"I'm supposed to be there for you."

"Yes, you are. But you weren't."

"You'd rather he was there than me!"

"When the Hell did I say that?" True, though it may have been.

"You should have sent him to wake me up!"

"Are you kidding me?" He was being completely irrational at this point and there is no way to combat that with a rational defense.

He banged his fist on the kitchen table. I jumped. We stood staring at each other for what felt like hours.

He finally broke the silence. "I'm going for a drive."

He slammed the door behind him. I laid on the couch and cried a little. I must have nodded off because it was a little after noon when I was woken up by my phone. It was Frank. Ian had text messaged her and told her what happened. She was calling on her lunch break.

"Oh, my God! Are you okay? Is the arm permanently damaged?"

"No. I'm all right. I'm pretty sore, but I'll live."

"Nerve damage?"

"None to the arm."

"You got lucky."

"I know it."

We spent the next half hour using the opportunity to get caught up. We hadn't heard each other's voices in ages and it felt so good to have an actual conversation with her. I missed her so much.

The rest of the day, I fielded text messages from Megan, Brian, and concerned coworkers in between drifting in and out of consciousness. This was my normal sleep time but I wasn't getting any rest with all of the interruptions.

Keith didn't return until that evening. He brought Chinese take-out. We ate in relative silence and I went to bed around 10 p.m. My office manager had told me not to even think about coming in for my shift that night and I was ridiculously tired anyway.

I had just laid my head on the pillow when I got the text message I didn't realize I had been waiting for.

"You still doing okay?" Ian's concern was audible as I read the message.

"Yes. Thank you for being there for me today."

"I will always be here for you."

Just Pissed: By Ian

    Okay. I don't know which pissed me off more; that Keith wasn't there for Suz when she needed him or that he was pissed at me for stepping up. Either way, fuck him. I left the hospital and showed up to my jobsite angry. I grabbed the spare jeans and boots I kept in my car and got dressed in the porta-john. I explained to my boss what happened and he asked if I wanted the day off to take care of her. I would have loved to have said 'yes' but I needed the money too badly and I knew Keith would have lost his fucking mind.

    I text messaged Frank and Megan to let them know that Suz was hurt but okay. I knew she wouldn't do it because she wouldn't want them worrying about her. She could yell at me for it later.

    I set to helping my coworkers dig out an old driveway so we could lay a brick one. The more I thought about Keith's attitude, the angrier I got and I'm pretty sure at one point I could have dug that driveway out with my bare hands without blinking. I worked passed my off time to make up the hours from that morning. I was sweaty, dirty, and exhausted.

    Eddie asked me if I was going to be okay. Yeah. Just fine. I was just pissed.

    I went home to my tiny apartment. I had gotten out most of my frustration at work and now I just wanted to calm down the rest of the way. I stripped down and threw my clothes on the couch. I turned on the shower hot enough that it probably could have melted my skin, but I didn't care. I stood there letting the water run over me and didn't notice that I wasn't alone.

    "Damn. My boyfriend's sexy." Megan's voice scared the shit out of me.

    The shower curtain was see-through and I could barely make out her shape by the door on the other side. Why was she here? I'm pretty sure we didn't have a date schedule for tonight.

    I pulled back the curtain. "I'll be out in a minute."

    She left the bathroom.

    I finished my shower and walked out in the living area with a towel around my waist.

Megan was sitting in a chair at the table. "You want to drop that towel?" She wiggled her eyebrows at me.

"Not today." I felt bad about rejecting her, but I was in no mood.

I got dressed behind the shoji she had insisted that I buy. I was sitting on the bed pulling up my socks when my stomach made a horrible noise like an angry animal. That's when I realized I hadn't eaten anything at all that day. I noticed something else, too. Something smelled delicious. I went out back towards where Megan was sitting. She had set the table and brought Italian take-out.

"Please, don't tell me I forgot an anniversary or Valentine's Day or something." I knew we didn't have a date scheduled.

"No. Can't a girl who can't cook just bring dinner to her man?" She stuck out her lower lip.

"I'm sorry. It's been a long day. Thank you." I sat across from her and she started portioning out the food.

"It's okay. What was so bad about today?"

"You mean aside from one of my best friends waking me up to tell me she almost lost her arm and needed me to meet her at the hospital?"

"You said she's going to be okay."

"She is but at the time I didn't know that. They did all kinds of scans and had to put her under to dig around in it. It was a lot."

"But she's going to be okay."

"Yeah."

"Then why are you upset?"

I thought for a moment but only one word came to mind, "Keith."

"I meant to ask why you were there instead of him."

"Because he's a dick who doesn't really care about his wife."

Megan stopped with a fork full of noodles halfway to her mouth. "Huh?"

"I called him. She called him. Her coworkers called him. He couldn't be bothered to answer the phone."

"He's a heavy sleeper."

Marie Joseph-Charles 193

"Then why did he stop by the gas station for smokes and energy drinks like he does EVERY morning? If he was worried, he should have come straight to the hospital."

"Well. Yeah."

"Would you be pissed if I knew you were hurt in the hospital but ran errands before coming to see you?"

"No doubt. I'd probably kill you!"

"You know what the frosting on that bullshit cake was?"

"What?" She seemed apprehensive about asking.

"He had the nerve to cop an attitude with me at the hospital. He looked at me like it was my fault he wasn't there for her and he was pissed that I was! How's that for a load of fucking shit? He should have been happy that someone was there for her!"

"Yeah but he was probably just jealous that you did his job."

"Being there for her isn't a job. He should have been there because he loves her. I was. She deserves better than that." I stabbed an olive in frustration.

Megan was quiet for a minute. "You really care about her, don't you?"

"Of course I do. She would take a bullet for me and I would do the same for her."

She kind of sighed and pushed the rest of her food away. "I see."

"I'm sorry. You don't need to hear me yelling about all of this. How was your day?"

She talked while I kept eating. She said something about a job offer in Dayton, but I was only half listening. After dinner, we watched TV on the couch until she fell asleep. I was still a little on edge though.

I text messaged Suzanne. *"You still ok?"*

"Yeah. Thank you for being there for me today."

I thought for a minute. *"I will always be here for you."*

She Didn't Have to Lie: By Ian

Women make my head hurt. Just when I think I've got one somewhat figured out, she'll throw me a fucking curve ball and I come to the realization that I know nothing.

It was November of '15. I was geared up to watch the UC game (basketball, of course). I had the nachos prepared and I was ready for Megan to come watch the came with me. I loved that my girlfriend wouldn't just let me watch the game, but actually joined in the fun of yelling at the refs, binging on nachos, and just forgetting about the outside world.

When she arrived, she wasn't her usual pre-game self. She looked at the couch and the coffee table piled with chicken and nachos.

"What's wrong?" I closed the door behind her.

She turned to face me. "Do you think we can go out tonight instead?"

"What? The game starts in, like, twenty minutes."

"I really don't feel like watching basketball."

My jaw about hit the floor.

She continued. "To be honest," she looked at the floor, "I really don't care for watching basketball at all."

"What the fuck?" Megan and I, I admit, had very little in common so for her to say she didn't enjoy the one thing that we actually *did* have in common kind of hit me like a fucking wrecking ball. "You've just pretended to like it for our entire relationship?"

"Kind of."

"Why?"

"I don't know. You like it so much and I like spending the time with you. We've always had such a hard time making time for each other and I didn't want to lose that."

I didn't know what to say. This was coming completely out of no where as far as I could tell.

"Are you mad?" She looked up at me.

I took a deep breath. Of course I was mad. She just admitted she had been lying about one of the core foundations of our relationship. You're damn right, I was mad! "Of course not."

Marie Joseph-Charles 195

She perked up. "Good!" She smiled. "What do you want to do for dinner?"

"I'm going to have nachos and chicken while watching the game."

Her smile completely vanished. "You just said-"

"I said I'm not mad. But I'm not going to change my plans last minute just because you did. I've been looking forward to this all week."

Her jaw dropped. "Fine!" She stormed out of the apartment and slammed the door behind her.

Don't judge me. She may not like basketball, but I do. Worst of all, she just admitted she had been lying for our entire fucking relationship. If she lied about something like that, what else had she been lying about?

I ended up not enjoying the game at all. I spent the whole time going back and forth between being pissed that she lied and feeling guilty that I had let her leave angry. I kept telling myself we both just needed time to cool off.

After the game, I sat in my bed and stared at the wall. I was starting go into that not-angry-not-sad-just-kind-of-numb place. I rubbed my eyes and looked over at my night stand. There was my sketchbook. I started to think about Suz. She wouldn't lie to me like that. At least, I didn't think she would. I put the book in my lap and ran my fingers over the leather. I don't know. It was somehow comforting. I opened it and looked at the last sketch I had worked on. The idea was that it would be for an office complex or even fancy apartments. I hadn't worked out the interior yet.

My phone buzzed. It was Frank. *"You mad at Megan."*

"Yup."

"You lied to her?"

"She lied to me."

"How long til you talk to her?"

"She got pissed and left. It's on her." I started feeling myself getting angry again.

"Okay. Try not to stay mad for too long. She only did it to spend time with you."

"She didn't have to lie."

Brian and the emotional affair by Suzanne

It was 2016. There was a rapid, sharp knock at my front door. It wasn't late but I was groggy and I stumbled to the door to open it. A gust of cold December air came in. Frank was there and she had obviously been crying for quite some time.

"Jesus Christ! What happened? And since when do you knock?"

"This one is more than a milk shake. I think I need to sit down."

"Of course! Of course! Come on in." I ushered her in and closed the door. I sat her on the couch. I ran to the kitchen to get her a drink of water.   I handed her the glass.

She took it gingerly. "Thank you."

"Now what is wrong?"

"It's Brian."

"Okay."

"He's having an affair."

"What?!" I was in complete disbelief. I didn't really like him but he never struck me as an adulterer.

"With the teenage boy next door."

"Wait. What? What the Hell?"

"I came home from work early to surprise him and found them having sex on the kitchen table. I saw them. I screamed. They screamed. And I left. I went to the day care. I grabbed the kids and dropped them off at Mom's on the way here."

"What the Hell?"

"The kid is nineteen so at least it's not illegal."

"Still! What the Hell?"

"Can you say anything other than that?"

"No! I really can't!"

"Well. I guess now I'm going to know how Keith feels when he finds out about you and Ian."

"Ian and I are not sleeping together."

"No. You're having an emotional affair. That's much worse."

I let those words sink in for a second. "Do you want to stay here for the night?"

Marie Joseph-Charles 198

"I really do."

"Come on. Keith's out of town and there's plenty of space."

"I knew this was the right place to come."

I took her to her old room and we got her settled in. I gave her one of Keith's t-shirts that he had gotten too heavy for to wear as a nightgown. I sat with her for awhile while she wept. She had almost soaked through the pillow before she finally fell asleep. I went back down to the kitchen and put a kettle on the stove. I needed a bit of tea after this. He was screwing the kid next door? What the Hell?

The next morning, we both woke up early. We sat in the kitchen with a mug of coffee each. She was still wearing Keith's t-shirt and it had new makeup stains from where she had been crying and wiped her face. We sat and sipped in silence for a few moments while she collected her thoughts and I let the caffeine kick in.

"So what's next?" I didn't really have anything comforting to say.

"I guess now I become a statistic."

"What do you mean?"

"I need to find a lawyer and a new place to live."

"You should probably get the house and make him move but I was referring to the more immediate future."

"I don't want the house. Too many memories. I'm going to call in at work and let them know I'll be out for a few days and they need to find a relief vet while I get things in order. Mom doesn't work on Sundays so I'm sure she won't mind keeping the kids for the day so I can go back and probably confront him."

"Do you need back up?"

She smiled. "No. But I may need a place to crash for a while."

"That room is always yours. It may be hard to fit three kids in it, but this is your home too."

Tears welled up in her eyes. "Thank you." She choked them back with another big swig of coffee.

I got to work at eight and worked my typical, chaotic Sunday shift. At 11p.m. I stumbled in my front door, hungry and exhausted. Something smelled amazing! Keith shouldn't have been home yet, not that he could cook anyway. I stepped in the kitchen and Frank was setting the table.

"What's all this? I sat down and she poured me a glass of chardonnay.

"A 'thank-you' to my best friend for letting me ruin her pillowcase and husband's shirt and a celebration spaghetti."

"Celebration?"

She set a plate of noodles and sauce in front of me and sat down while pouring wine for herself. "Today was a productive day."

I chased a huge bite of spaghetti with wine. I was so hungry. "Explain."

"When I got home, I was packing clothes for me and the kids. I really didn't have a plan but I knew we couldn't stay there. Well, he came home as I was leaving and I was so proud of myself for not crying in front of him!"

After gulping down bread and chasing with more wine. "What happened?!"

She topped off my glass. "He looked at me and says 'divorce?' I said 'yup.' He said 'can we talk about it?' I said 'in court.' And I got in my car and left!"

"You just left everything?"

"I'll go back for more later. I don't want to make this separation or divorce into a big deal. I want the kids and he can see them. I want their clothes and toys and I want some money every month to make sure they're fed and have a roof over their heads."

I had almost finished my plate by this time. "What about all of your stuff?"

"It's just stuff and most of it is tied to memories of him. I don't want to forget him. That's kind of hard when two of the kids look exactly like him."

I kind of giggled. Both Frank and Brian were blonde-haired and blue-eyed and so were all three kids so I thought they all looked like both of them. "So do you have a plan?"

"Well, that's how my day was productive. I talked to Mom and she's going to let me turn the basement into a little apartment for me and the kids for a little while while things get sorted out. I already started the process to get the kids enrolled in daycare and preschool and I submitted my resume at a few places nearby."

"So you're coming home? I thought you'd stay in Indy so the kids could stay with their friends."

"They're young. They will make new friends easily and Chad is still an infant. I guess in the two-hour drive there and the two hours back, it just kind of came to me. Where do I always go when I need something? Indy was home but it was never *home*. I grew up here and I don't see why my kids shouldn't too."

"I can't believe it. You're actually coming home?"

"I'm coming home." She smiled.

She got up and took my plate and filled it with more spaghetti. We spent the rest of dinner talking about job opportunities and what we needed to do to make things happen.

The following week, Frank went back to work on Wednesday and commuted to and from Indy. Her plan was to continue to until she found something closer to home. She found a sitter until the kids could start daycare and preschool and Cathy dropped them off and picked them up. She was an awesome grandma and I think she secretly hoped they would never move out. That weekend, Frank drove her car, I drove mine, and Ian drove a moving truck with Keith riding shotgun. We loaded up half of the kids' things (they were still going to be allowed to see Brian so we didn't leave him with nothing), all of Frank's things (how many clothes does one person really need?), and the basement living area furniture (it was far less used and cheaper so Brian couldn't complain). It took most of the day but it surprisingly went without confrontation. Brian spent most of the day skulking and watching to make sure we didn't intentionally break any of his things.

The divorce itself went relatively smoothly. Frank asked for exactly what she said and he agreed with minimal fuss. When they filed for an annulment, they had to see a marriage counselor and that's where things got weird. Apparently, Brian wasn't gay or even bi. He had some kind of alpha-male issues (which we kind of already knew) and he married an alpha female. Whatever Frank said was law in their household. His way of 'reaffirming his masculinity' (for his own pride) was to dominate other males. What the Hell? Right? He had issues.

Space in a Relationship: By Ian

It was a Sunday in January of '17 and I was off of work early. There isn't really much landscaping work in the Midwest in the winter.

I text messaged Megan, *"Hey! I'm off early if you are up for hanging out or something."*

She responded, *"I don't really feel up to going out."*

"Do you want me to come over and make you something to eat and maybe watch a movie?"

"No. I just want some alone time."

I had a sudden shock of panic. *"Okay. Maybe next time."*

"Yeah maybe"

Ladies, let me tell you something. When you say you need 'space' or 'alone time' it does nothing less than trigger a state of sheer fucking terror in a man. What could I have possibly done wrong? Was she just having a bad day? I was freaking out and got into my car. Driving without a destination was kind of a bad habit of mine when I was upset.

I drove passed Keith and Suzanne's house. Suzanne's car wasn't out front but Keith's was. I kept driving. I don't know why but I really didn't want to talk to him. I headed towards Mom's house. I didn't care if Karen had inherited it. It was still Mom's house.

Fifteen minutes doesn't last long when you're in panic mode. I pulled in across the street at Cathy and Steve's. I got out of my car and looked across the street at my former home. The lawn hadn't been cared for. Mom's prized flower bed was completely messed up. There were toys and bikes all over the yard. It hurt to see it like that.

I turned back to Cathy's house. Before I could knock on the door, it opened quickly and Frank came out.

"Jesus! You scared the shit out of me!" I almost fell off the porch.

"Let's go!" She walked passed me in a hurry.

"Where are we going?" I had to walk quickly to get behind her.

"Hardware store. I need out of this house."

Marie Joseph-Charles 203

"What's wrong?"

"Mom. She's so happy about me and the kids moving in. She's driving me crazy."

"Ha! Where are the kids?" I got in the passenger side of her minivan.

"Nonno- my dad- took them to the play area at Union Terminal so I could work on getting things set up in the basement. Mom decided she needed to help me and has been going on and on about how great it is to have her whole family back together and that we may need to figure out how to put walls up down there so the kids can have their own rooms-"

"It's not that big down there."

"No kidding! Plus, this is supposed to be TEMPORARY! I am *not* living with my parents until my kids are adults!"

I laughed. "So why are we going to the hardware store?"

"I need shelves to put the kids' books and stuff on."

"Why are we really going?"

"So I don't commit matricide." She pulled into a parking space and shut off the minivan. "So what were you doing at our house anyway?"

"Megan needed space." I shut the van door kind of hard behind me.

She stopped dead in her tracks and looked me in the eye. "What did you do?"

"Nothing! Nothing that I know of, at least."

"Think hard."

We were going in the big sliding doors. "I haven't been able to go out much because of this stupid project I've been working on. That's why I tried to take her to dinner tonight."

"That wouldn't be it. Megan's too pragmatic to let your school work upset her."

"Then I really don't know. Why do women have to be so difficult?"

Frank laughed. We were looking over decorative shelving and she was touching them each in turn. "Women are really simple. That's what makes us difficult."

I scoffed. "Okay. Care to explain that one?"

"All women want is to feel like they matter. The degree to which they want that feeling may vary from woman to woman, but in the end, that's all we want. Men can't grasp this simplicity. They have to do everything the hard way."

"So you're saying the only reason women are difficult is because we make them difficult."

"Exactly."

We were looking at shelving brackets now. "For example?"

"Going out."

"Okay…"

"How often have you said something like 'Hey, I'm off on Sunday if you want to do something' and then gotten frustrated when she wouldn't pick something to do?"

"All the fucking time."

"Okay. And I'll bet you text it instead of having the decency to call her."

"What's your point?"

"So, first of all, calling shows her you took the time out of your day and that you wanted to hear her voice. Second of all, saying something like '*if you want*' makes her sound like an after thought. It's like the only reason you want to spend time with her is because you have nothing else to do."

"That's not it. I wouldn't be asking if I didn't want to spend time with her."

"Then why don't you say that?"

"Say what?"

"That you want to spend time with her."

I was getting frustrated. "That's what I did!"

"No. You said you have some free time if she'd like to fill it."

"So what should I say?"

"Something more like, 'I'm off on Sunday and I'd like to hang out with you.' By saying that, she is no longer an afterthought. She is important."

"I kind of see where you're going with this."

"Good. Keep following along. Now. Let me guess. When you want to eat out, you always try to let her pick the place."

"Of course. I'm giving her control."

Frank sighed. "She doesn't want control. She wants value. Can you hear the difference between 'Hey, I'm off on Sunday if you want to do something' and then getting mad when she won't pick something to do *and* 'I'm off on Sunday and I'd like to BLANK or BLANK with you' ?"

"Women read too much into things."

"No. We just want one thing. If you know leaving your dirty underwear on the doorknob upsets her, show her she matters by not doing it. If she wants to go antiquing and you would rather take a power drill to your temple, do it anyway because I guarantee she has done plenty of things for you that she hated. None of these things hurt you and they show that she is important to you by making her things important. The problem is men doing lots of things like *that* or not picking up after themselves and leaving it for us or not listening and then getting mad when they say they don't know what we want but we are *blatantly* telling them-"

"Whoa. Whoa. Whoa. Are we still talking about my relationship with Megan or…"

"All relationships. You and Megan. Suz and Keith. Me and Brian. We just want to feel like we matter and you guys think we want jewelry and gifts. Gifts are nice when they're called for but what we really want can't be bought. "

"You did- and still do- matter to Brian. That's why he cheated on you."

"That's an oxymoronic statement."

"But it's not. He could have found a submissive breeder to marry like the rest of his family. He could have married someone who would shut up and make babies. But he didn't. He chose you out of love but your strength and that fucked up family of his made him feel like less of a man. Instead of leaving you for a more, um, domesticated woman, he found a different way to cope."

She was paying the cashier for the shelves and brackets. "I'm not saying I don't understand why Brian did what he did. I wish he had taken up hunting or something else to make him feel more like a man, but it is how every other mammalian species shows dominance and I get that on a primal level. I just wish he had shown that I matter by talking to me about it instead of fucking the kid next door."

It always shocked me to hear Frank cuss. "I get it. Communication is hard."

"It shouldn't be."

"But it is."

"I think you need to go communicate with your girlfriend and find out what you did wrong."

Goodbye Megan: By Ian

It was another couple of days before Megan contacted me. I had wanted to text her, go to her apartment, or maybe show up at her work. I didn't understand why she was mad at me or even *if* she was mad at me. I really just wanted to know what the fuck was going on. She had a key to my apartment and I noticed that she had come in while I was gone and picked up some of her things.

It was a Saturday night. I was dead tired. I had stayed up all night Friday trying to get this project for school done. That morning, we started laying a brick driveway at eight in the morning and we didn't finish until after nine at night. I stood in my shower and let the hot water run down me. My muscles were sore and I could barely keep my eyes open. I heard my phone *ding*. I looked through the shower curtain at my phone on the bathroom sink. Fuck. I had a text message. I turned off the shower and dried off my hands.

My heart lit up and I was suddenly awake. It was from Megan. *"Meet me at Brooker's for drinks?"*

I messaged back, *"I'll be there in thirty."*

I jumped back in the shower. I needed to make sure I was scrubbed clean. I hadn't seen or heard from her in so long. It was like first date jitters all over again.

Brooker's was a tiny little hole-in-the-wall karaoke bar in Northern Kentucky. If you weren't friends with someone who knew it, you would never find it. My cousin was the owner. I got there before she did. I sat at the bar with a glass of tap light. I was nervous and I couldn't understand why. Then I saw her.

She didn't look like herself. She looked like she hadn't slept in days. She was pale and sad. She was wearing a baggy sweatshirt and looked kind of sick. She didn't smile when she sat down next to me.

"Hi." That's it. That was all I could say.

"Hi." She didn't look at me when she said it.

"How have you been?"

"Not very good."

I had a really bad feeling about asking. "What's wrong?"

Marie Joseph-Charles 208

She took a deep breath and when she exhaled she was kind of shaking. "I've been doing a lot of thinking."

"About?" I had a feeling I knew where this was going.

"Us."

"What have you been thinking?" I took a big gulp of my beer just so I would have something to swallow.

"Maybe we shouldn't be an 'us' anymore."

I think my heart just stopped. "You mean you want to break up."

She looked at the floor and started to cry a little. "Yeah."

"Why? Why are you doing this? You wouldn't be crying if you wanted to." I grabbed both of her hands.

She pulled them away from me. "I don't want to. I *have* to."

What the fuck? "What do you mean you *have* to?"

"I want things for myself that I'm not getting from my life with you."

"Like what?"

She looked up at me. "You."

"What does that mean? You have me."

"No, I don't. Not completely. I love you. And I know you love me. But in the end, your heart just isn't in it and I need someone who will give his heart to me completely."

"I really have no idea what the fuck you are talking about."

"I know you don't now. But you will." She stood up and pushed my key into my palm. She kissed me and started to cry harder. "Goodbye, Architect."

That was it. She left. She walked out of the bar and out of my life. I was left with absolutely zero understanding of what had just happened.

I heard a glass slide across the bar. I looked and it was a scotch. The bartender looked at me. "You need this, man." I didn't even hesitate.

Marie Joseph-Charles 209

It will stop hurting: By Suzanne

It was late on a Saturday. I was coming off of second shift and it was about two in the morning. I got a phone call.

"Suz! You come 'n get me?" Ian sounded blitzed out of his mind.

"Where are you?"

"Brooker's. My cousin isn't here to drive me home."

"I'll be there as soon as I can." I hung up wondering why he hadn't called Megan.

It was about a forty minute drive to Brooker's from the clinic. He was sitting outside the little bar, leaned up against the wall of the building with his eyes closed.

I parked the car and got out. "You dead?"

"No, but I wish I was."

I sat down on the ground next to him. He smelled like about eight different boozes and I probably could have lit his breath with a match. He leaned his head over on my shoulder.

"What happened, Love?" I could tell through the alcohol-soaked facial expression that he was upset.

"I'm not entirely sure."

"Well, what are you sure of?"

"Megan's gone."

My heart skipped a beat. "What do you mean she's 'gone'?"

He held out his apartment key. "I don't think she will change her mind."

I couldn't believe it. Megan and Ian were a couple to be envious of (at least from my perspective.) Why would she just up and leave? They had been together for so long.

I tried to look down at him. "Did she say why?"

"My heart just isn't in it!" He sounded almost mocking and he grabbed his chest and mimed releasing his heart like a bird. "I don't know where my heart is but right now I'm sure it's not beating."

"It is. It's just kind of numb right now."

"Why does numb hurt so much?"

"I don't know, Love. But I promise it will stop hurting."

Marie Joseph-Charles 210

"Not before my head hurts from the hangover I'm going to have tomorrow."

I smiled a little and laid my head on top of his. "Probably not."

"Suz?"

"Yeah?"

"Can we sit like this for a little while?"

"Everything is spinning, huh?"

"Well, yeah. But this is really nice right now."

"Okay. Just don't pass out on me. There's no way I can drag you to the car."

"That's fair."

We sat like that, on the ground outside the bar, for almost an hour. I think he was trying not to cry but I couldn't see his face. When he thought he could walk, I helped him into my car. I took him home with me and set him up on the couch. He passed out almost instantly. Keith was pissed that Ian had called me instead of him but I shrugged it off. My friend needed me. I took off his shoes and covered him with a blanket from the hall closet. I ran my hand over his forehead before I turned out the light and went to bed.

A Mouse in a Trap: By Suzanne

It was June of the same year Megan left. Keith and I had
had yet another big fight. He was angry that I was going to be
working on the day of his family reunion. He said that I was only
doing it to avoid his family. I kept trying to explain that it wasn't
my fault that I was on a shift rotation and his family had decided to
throw this thing together last minute. He had called me a liar and a
coward. I left in tears.

I pulled myself together as I pulled into my dad's driveway.
I didn't want him to see me crying but I really didn't know where
else to go; all of my friends were working. I took a deep breath as
I stood on the front porch. Before I had a chance to exhale, the
door flew open.

"Button!" My dad smile wide.

I exhaled a little more out of frustration than trying to
collect myself. "Don't call me that."

He ignored me. "Come in! You're just in time for tea! No
jokes about me being an old woman."

I kind of smiled. My grandmother was a stickler for a four
o'clock tea time and had drilled that into her children. We sat at
the kitchen table.

"What kind would you like?" Dad opened a drawer that
contained the largest assortment of teas you could ask for.

"Oolong. And honey."

"Ever the caffeine addict. I've found this great green tea
you should try."

"I hate green tea. And black tea so don't even try."

"Button. You don't know you don't like something unless
you try it."

I rolled my eyes. "Okay Grandma."

He shot me an evil look as he dropped the steel tea ball into
a mug and set in front of me with a jar of honey. I kind of lost
myself a little as I swirled the tea ball around by the chain and
watched the water darken.

"Suzanne. Are you going to tell me what's wrong?"

He rarely ever actually called me by my name. I looked up.
He was staring at me with something between concern and
eagerness.

"Who said anything was wrong?" I held my mug up and
blew the steam.

"Suzanne Elizabeth. No games."

First and middle. Oh, dear Lord. I took a big gulp of the
hot tea. It wasn't a very effective stall tactic but it was something.
"I don't know how much longer I can stay married to Keith."

"Forever."

"I'm serious, Dad. He and I can barely stand each other.
He's always yelling at me and making me feel bad."

"Well, Button, maybe you should find out what's really
bothering him. Maybe then you'll understand why he's taking it
out on you."

Really? "Dad. It shouldn't matter. He shouldn't be taking
anything out on me. That's not the way a relationship works."

"Maybe you two should try counseling."

"He won't go. He won't go to any kind of doctor."

"Well, Button, you need to figure it out."

"Honestly, I don't think he really loves me. I kind of
wonder if he ever did."

"That's the biggest load of nonsense I've ever heard. Of
course he loves you. He's just stressed out. You need to be there
for him."

I really couldn't believe what I was hearing. "When was
the last time you were there for Angela?"

"That's different. I do love your mother, just not the same
way I used to. Marriage isn't about romance. It's about securing a
future. Raising children and taking care of each other. Everything
else is just a bonus."

"What?" Is he really saying what I think he's saying?

"What are you saying? That you want to divorce Keith?"

"Kind of. Yes."

"'Til death do you part.' Not 'til divorce do you part'"

"Really? When you talked me into this whole marriage
thing, you said divorce was an option."

"He's not beating you or giving you a real reason to leave. You just aren't happy right now. Change things up a little. Find a way to be happy."

"You cannot be serious."

"You have a good arrangement. Let's face it, you can't pay your bills without him. You don't have children so you won't get much in alimony. You need him for survival. Find a way to make it work or you'll have to wait until he's dead to collect the insurance money."

"Wow. Thank you for the pragmatism, Dad. I think I had better go now." I stood up.

"Button-"

"No!"

No sooner had I backed out of the driveway when BOOM! I started sobbing uncontrollably. The one person who should have understood me; who should have wanted to protect me. No. He didn't care how I felt. I suddenly felt like I had been tricked into this marriage. I was a mouse who succumbed to the lure of free cheese and SNAP! I was trapped and slowly dying with no one to save me.

Love vs Being in Love by Ian

We were sitting on the back porch at Cathy and Steve's house in August. The sun was going down and the sky was pink. Amber and Christina were playing in the grass. Amber was delegating the rules for the lightning bug game. I couldn't help but laugh as she carefully laid it out for her sister who was eagerly holding her pickle jar. Leave it to Frank to give birth to a little girl who, at barely four years old, already wanted to be president and was delegating to her underlings. I had Chad sleeping in my lap so Frank could have a little break. Looking down at him, I suddenly realized that there was a part of me that didn't want to be a dad. How could I be responsible for another life? I was over thirty and didn't even have my own life in order.

I looked over at Frank. She was leaned back and rocking in a patio chair watching her girls.

"Remember that marriage pact we had when we were fifteen?" I asked.

She smiled a little. "No"

"'No,' you don't remember or 'no,' you won't marry me?"

"I think I'm done with the whole marriage bit for a while. Even if means turning down a great guy like you."

"I'm just getting shot down left and right lately."

"I won't lie, I kind of miss Megan."

A little piece of my heart hurt when I heard her name. "Me too."

"I'll be honest though, I don't really blame her for moving on."

I turned to face her. "What do you mean?"

"She told you your heart wasn't in it, right?"

"Yeah."

"I get that. It took you *how long* before you told her you loved her?"

"That's not something that should get thrown around lightly."

"You wouldn't move in with her."

"I'd never lived on my own and I didn't think I would be a good roommate after Mom died."

Marie Joseph-Charles 215

She kind of sighed and sat up. "You really are an idiot."

"What did I do?"

"You love Megan. We all know that. But you aren't *in love* with Megan. She knew that and she was tired of waiting for you to fall *in* love with her."

"What's the difference?"

"Loving someone just means that you will always do what you can for them. You are happy to have them as part of your life. You would be devastated without them. Being *in love* means all of that but you also want to share your life with them."

"I did share my life with her."

"No, you did stuff with her like you do stuff with me- minus the bedroom stuff of course- but you didn't share your life with her."

"How? I told her everything that happened every day."

"That's not exactly it."

I was getting irritated. "What then?"

"What book do you keep on your nightstand? Who was the first person you told when your mom chose hospice? Where was the first place you went when you were pissed at your sister when your mom died? Who did you call when Megan left?"

I opened my mouth, but I suddenly realized what she was saying. Fuck. It all went back to Suzanne. I could have defended every one of those arguments. I like to draw before I went to bed, that's why I kept the sketchbook on the night stand. I didn't mean to tell Suz about my mom in hospice; I had just gone there because I knew they would be home and I needed a distraction. I didn't go to Megan's house when Mom died because she had been there *when* mom died. I could have argued, but I knew it was pointless. She was right. It all lead back to Suzanne.

I guess my face gave me away. Frank got a smirk and leaned back in her chair. "That's wanting to share your life."

I felt a little defeated. The baby shifted so I leaned him up against my chest and rubbed his back. "Now what?"

"What do you mean?"

"What should I do?"

"Well, you could tell her how you feel."

"I really don't like that option."

"You could kill Keith and make it look like an accident. Slay the dragon and save the girl."

I laughed a little. "Are you calling Keith a dragon?"

She looked serious. "Let's be honest. He's a far cry from the guy we grew up with. He controls her and I don't know if she realizes it or not."

"Have you said something to her?"

"Kind of. I really want them to figure it out on their own. I don't want to take sides but…"

"But, what?"

"Let's face it. He's not going to let her go. He'd rather they were both miserable than let her find happiness with another man. That chick in California really did a number on him and he doesn't let things go."

She was right. There was no way Keith was going to let her go. I knew Suz was strong enough to leave him if she felt like she had someone to back her up but he would destroy her and leave her in pieces in the process.

Frank could read my mind. "He'll destroy her. You can say it. We both think of Keith as a brother, but I think we are clinging to the guy we grew up with. He isn't him anymore."

"No. No, he's not."

The kids came running up. Christina was crying and holding her head and Amber was defending herself. "She had one on her head! I was just trying to catch it."

"Good, Lord. You two!" Frank picked up Christina and carried her in the house. "You can put the baby in his crib now!" She yelled at me over her shoulder.

I carried little Chad down the stairs to the makeshift basement apartment and laid him in his crib. After I put him down, I stood straight and cracked my back. I stretched (hadn't moved much since the kid fell asleep on me) and looked up. That's when I saw it. On a shelf, high above the crib where the kids couldn't reach, tucked behind a stuffed lamb, was a bottle of time release caffeine pills. I guess Frank was having trouble being a full-time veterinarian and a full-time mom. I thought about all those energy drinks and pop cans in Keith's car. Caffeine addict to the point that it barely phased him. That's when I had a really bad thought.

I got the bottle down and looked at it. *Take ½ to 1 caplet not more often than every 3 to 4 hours. The recommended dose of this product contains about as much caffeine as a cup of coffee. Limit the use of caffeine-containing medications, foods, or beverages while taking this product because too much caffeine may cause nervousness, irritability, sleeplessness, and, occasionally, rapid heart beat. In severe overdoses, death has been reported.* I had read news reports where people had died from caffeine overdoses. With as much as Keith already consumed, would it really be hard for him to overdose with a couple of these? No one would think twice about an overweight caffeine addict who smokes and ended up having a heart attack. If they questioned the amount of caffeine in his system at autopsy, all they would have to do was look in his car and there would be the answer. What was I thinking? I couldn't kill someone! I put the bottle back on the shelf. I don't know what happened. It was like my hands had a mind of their own. I got the bottle back down, put a couple of the tablets in my pocket, and hid the bottle back behind the lamb before I left. *Slay the dragon.*

Proof of Ownership: By Suzanne

     In October of 2017, I walked in the front door. I was exhausted, as usual. I set my bag on the floor and looked around. There were no less than six half-drunk soda cans lying around. The sofa pillows were on the floor (that hadn't been swept). I walked into the kitchen. There were scummy dishes piled in the sink (presumably because the dishwasher hadn't been emptied). The garbage can was overflowing and smelled awful. There were boot prints all over the floor and something brown dried on the counter tops. I tried to keep it together as I doubled back and went down the hall to the bedroom to undress for a shower. I wished I hadn't done that. Clothes were EVERYWHERE. The hardwood floor was covered by a carpet of socks, shirts, and pants. The blankets were balled up in the middle of the bed with Ariel sitting on top. I lost it. He had been home off of work for three days and, not only had he not done a single chore, he had completely trashed the house. I was coming off of a fourteen hour day after only six hours of sleep. I was exhausted and the house was disgusting. I crumpled to the floor and began sobbing. Ariel hopped off the bed and came to comfort me.

     I heard boot steps behind me. "I thought I heard you pull up. What's for dinner?" I sobbed loudly. "Woah. Calm down. You don't have to cook. We can order in."

     I kept crying. "I'm not hungry."

     "Okay. Well. I'll order some pizza and put some in the fridge for you for later if you want." He left.

     I continued crying. Ariel head butted me and purred as best he could. He had gotten old so he wasn't as loud as he had once been, but he tried. We sat on the clothes on the floor together until I had regained enough composure to go to the shower. My towel was gone. I stepped back out to the linen closet in the hall and grabbed the last clean one. I went back into the bathroom and shut the door. I stepped over the pile of laundry near the door. I stripped down and threw my clothes on top of the toilet, away from the boxer shorts on the floor that appeared to have a fecal stain on them.

Marie Joseph-Charles 219

I got in the tub and turned the shower on full heat. What the hell has happened to my life? My house has never been this disgusting. I've never been this exhausted. I've never been this *unhappy*. All that crap he spewed at our wedding about me being at his side was just bullshit. We weren't a team. I wasn't standing next to him. His days off were for him to enjoy. All of my free time was to be devoted to taking care of the house, running errands, or catering to him. I didn't get a day off. I didn't get to paint or hike nearly as much as he got to be in the garage. I wanted life. I wanted to LIVE. I didn't want to work, sleep, clean, and die.

When I got out of the shower, I wrapped myself in the towel. I went back to the bedroom and sat next to Ariel in the bed and put my face in my hands.

Boot steps. "Hey. You okay? Tired?"

I looked at him. He was completely oblivious. He was perfectly happy living in his own filth. "What are we doing?"

He looked confused. "What do you mean?"

"This. Us. What are we doing?"

He sat on the bed and tried to put his arm around me. I moved away from him. I suddenly became aware of just how long I had resented his touch.

He looked hurt for a millisecond and it was quickly replaced with anger. "You never want me to touch you any more."

"I know."

"Why? You don't want me to touch you. You don't want to talk to me any more."

"You get mad at me so fast when I try to talk to you. Any time I try to talk to you, you take it as a personal attack. It's just easier not to ay anything at all."

"That's not how a marriage is supposed to work."

"Marriage? This isn't a marriage. At best, it's a partnership. A symbiotic relationship."

"That's what a marriage is supposed to be."

"No. It isn't."

"Then enlighten me." He stood up. He was getting more angry.

"You use me as a maid and cheap housing. I use your added income. We aren't in love any more."

"You don't love me?!"

"Of course I do. That's the only reason I've stayed this long."

"It's because of him, isn't it?"

I knew the answer, but I asked anyway. "Him who?"

"Ian. Who else?"

"What in the actual Hell are you talking about?"

"Don't think I don't see the way you two look at each other. I know he keeps that book you got him right next to his bed. There has been something going on between you two for years, even if it's not physical."

I suddenly remembered the words 'emotional affair.' I didn't have time to dwell on that. "Are you out of your mind?"

"What then?!" He threw his arms in the air.

"I'm tired of living in your filth. If I don't clean, the house ends up like this!" I gestured around the room. "On top of working sixty hours a week. But you. You have had three days off and have done nothing around the house."

"All you have to do is tell me what needs to be done and I'll help."

"This isn't about HELPING. We are MARRIED. This is our HOME. At what point are you no longer helping me with chores and actually doing YOUR PART because YOU LIVE HERE TOO? You are thirty-five years old going on fifteen. You have no sense of responsibility."

"So you're questioning our marriage because I don't clean? Sorry!" He threw his hands in the air again.

"You don't get it. How many times have I asked you not to leave stuff on the kitchen counters because it triggers my anxiety attacks? How many times have I tried to confront you about your health? How many times have tried to talk to you about our dead sex life? I'm not questioning our marriage because you don't clean. I'm doing it because you have no respect for me at all. Your solution every time we have a problem is to ignore it and hope it goes away. Well my concerns are the problem and the only way they go away is if I do."

Marie Joseph-Charles 221

It was as if I saw something inside of him snap. He grabbed my wrist and yanked me to my feet. The towel fell to the floor around my ankles. He twisted my hand around and I heard something in my wrist crack and pop.

"See this?" He jammed my wedding ring at my face. "This means you're mine and I own you! You aren't going anywhere!"

He shoved me backwards and I fell to the ground. I heard his heavy steps and then the front door open and slam. I lay naked on the floor in the dirty laundry. I wanted to cry some more. But no tears came. I had nothing left inside me at that point. I was just an empty shell.

Broken Wrist; Broken Heart: By Suzanne

My wrist was turning colors and swelling. I was sure it was broken. I swallowed back the tears that I thought were in there (though I never felt them) and tried to regain my composure as I headed to work to radiograph it and confirm. There was no workman's comp this time and human hospitals are expensive. I was going to have to fix this on my own.

My phone started to buzz in the passenger seat. It was Ian. I hit the speaker phone and tried to control my voice. "Hello?"

"Hey! Are you okay? I just got off the phone with Keith and he said you two got into a pretty bad argument."

I looked at my purpling arm. "Yeah. I'm okay though."

"No, you're not. Where are you?"

"Heading into the clinic to get some things."

"I'll be there in twenty." He hung up before I could argue.

Thankfully the clinic wasn't too busy. I told the girls I hurt my wrist falling. They helped me set up the x-ray machine and take the radiographs. I was studying the images and trying to decide how to set it when one of them brought Ian back.

"Is that a human arm?"

He had come up behind me. I turned to face him and he saw my wrist as I stabilized it against an ice pack on my belly. "Jesus fucking Christ! What the fuck happened?" He gingerly moved my arm to get a better look. The icepack fell to the floor.

"I… I fell." I couldn't look him in the eye. The idea of lying to him was humiliating.

He lifted my chin and looked into my eyes. "Did he do this to you?"

I looked down at the floor. I could feel him shaking. Rage?

"I'm going to have a talk with him." He turned to leave.

I grabbed his arm with my good hand. "Don't, Love. It'll only make things worse."

He took my hand in his and kissed it. He looked me in the eyes. "You don't deserve this." He squeezed my hand and left.

I knew the girls had heard every bit of that and knew what really happened. I think they knew I was embarrassed because none of them said anything about it as they helped me set and splint my wrist. As they bandaged, I kept thinking about the mess that I was in. I was married to a man who had broken my wrist and told me he owned me. One of my best friends was out to defend me and, no doubt, when Frank found out, she would be too.

I looked at where Ian had kissed my good hand. I smiled a little on the inside. He'd kissed me. I didn't even have a chance to enjoy it or hug him or kiss him. I wanted nothing more than for him to be holding me right that moment. Why did I want to do those things? Oh, God. What had Frank said? An emotional affair. I loved him. Oh, my God. I loved him. I had no idea what do to with this realization but I knew it had to be put on the back burner for how.

I didn't want to go home. How could I keep living like this? Especially now that I knew who and what I really wanted. How was I going to get out? I procrastinated by checking the pharmacy closet for something to help the pain. I wasn't stupid enough to get into the controlled substances and I knew ibuprofen and icepacks would only go so far. As I scanned the shelves, I saw an open case of potassium chloride. In large enough doses, it can cause a cardiac response that looks similar to a heart attack. It's not an uncommon form of euthanasia in animals. My wheels started turning. Would anyone really be surprised if someone with Keith's physique and lifestyle had a heart attack? But how could I administer it? Maybe a little isoflourane in his CPAP so he'd sleep through the injection. No. I wouldn't need it. That man could sleep through the roof being torn off in a tornado. What was I thinking? I couldn't just kill my husband. I was just ruminating out of anger.

As I went to close the closet door, I looked own at my wrist and at my rings. *This means you're mine and I own you.* I put two of the bottles of KCl in my pocket.

I Promised Her at Her Wedding: By Ian

I was sitting at home. With no Megan, no school, and no
work that day, I had no idea how to occupy my time. I was bored
and lacking inspiration for my building designs. I tried playing
video games but I got bored with that too. I called Keith.

"What the fuck do you want?" He sounded pissed and I
could hear traffic in the background.

"Woah. Easy. I just wanted to see if you had anything to
work on on the car today."

"No. And I don't know if I'll be wanting your help any
time soon."

"What's your problem?"

"Suzanne and I got into a fight and I really don't want to
deal with her or your shit right now."

"Wow. Okay then." I hung up and instantly called
Suzanne.

"Hello?" Her voice was shaky.

"Hey! You all right? I just got off the phone with Keith
and he said you two got into a bad fight."

There was a pause. "I'm okay."

"No, you're not. Where are you?"

"Heading into the clinic to get some stuff."

"I'll be there in twenty minutes." She sounded awful and I
had to check on her. Nothing could have prepared me for what I
saw when I got there.

I threw on my shoes and ran out to my car. The clinic
where she worked wasn't too far of a drive. When I got there, one
of her assistants took me back through the employee's only area
where she was in a small room.

I looked at the computer screen she was staring at. I'd
broken a few bones in my life and I knew what that was. "Isn't
that human?"

I think I startled her. She turned to face me. Holy shit!
Her arm! It was purple and she was holding an ice pack on it.
"What the fuck happened?" I tried to get a better look at her arm.

"I fell."

Bullshit. I knew she was lying. She never lied to me. I put my hand on her face and she looked up at me. "Did he do this?"

She looked away from me again. My blood was boiling. Are you fucking kidding me? He hurt her. SERIOUSLY hurt her. No. There was no way this was going to slide. "I'm going to have to talk to him."

"No. It'll only make things worse."

I kissed her hand. I made her a promise at her wedding and I intended to keep it. I had seen him put her through some serious shit, but this was the final straw.

I got in my car and left. I knew he wasn't at his house and I wasn't sure how I was going to find him. But I was going to find him. *I might get arrested today.* I drove passed Frank's driveway. He wasn't there. I checked a few of his favorite bars. No luck.

The more I drove, the more I started to become a kind of scary calm. Okay. I find him. I hospitalize him for a few days. Maybe weeks if I can hit him with my car. Then what? He comes home and makes Suzanne take care of him. She will still be his prisoner and he may hurt her again.

I ran through scenario after scenario and they all ended up the same. Then, I remembered the caffeine pills. I could make this all go away. Free Suzanne for good. Slay the dragon. Frank was right. He wasn't the Keith we loved anymore and I knew I could never forgive him for hurting her.

I started thinking. I could invite him out for a late dinner or a drink or two and slip them to him. By the time they took effect, he'd have a heart attack at home, possibly in bed. No one would be able to link anything back to me.

He Was Really Gone: By Suzanne

I finally forced myself to go home. Keith wasn't there yet, despite it being late. I wandered into the bedroom to get a clean pair of pajamas. I took the potassium chloride out of my pocket. I tucked it in my nightstand drawer. Just in case. I showered as best I could without getting my splint wet. I fed the cat and made myself a sandwich. My adrenaline was full tilt when I finally laid down around one in the morning. About half an hour later, I heard the front door open and lock. He came in the bedroom. I felt him looking at me. Oh, God. Was he going to yell? Was he going to hit me? I pretended to be asleep.

He lay down next to me. He stunk of alcohol and body odor. I didn't dare move. He strapped his CPAP to his face and turned away from me.

Sometime after two, I heard him screaming. I sat upright and saw him clutching his chest. I stared at him for a few seconds before I realized what was actually happening. I set down the syringe and reached for my phone and dialed nine one one.

When the paramedics came, I called Frank, Ian, and his parents. We all met at the hospital. Frank was crying and rocking. Keith's parents were outside smoking. Ian and I were avoiding eye contact from opposing chairs.

As if a switch has been flipped, Frank stopped crying and looked at me. "What happened to your arm?"

"Broke my wrist."

Her eyes narrowed. "How?"

"Did something stupid." It wasn't a lie, entirely. Arguing with Keith was never smart.

She looked over at Ian and he nodded his head. "Oh, fuck him!" She stood up just as Keith's parents came back in and the doctor stepped out of the hall where they were working on him.

We all stood and faced the doctor. He shook his head. "I'm sorry."

Frank gasped and put her hands to her mouth. She looked from me to Ian. Somehow, I think she knew.

Keith's mom started crying and threw her arms around me. I didn't like the woman but I allowed it. Truthfully, I was kind of numb. It really happened. He was gone.

I made eye contact with Ian for the first time. We just
seemed to understand completely. We both knew what happened.
And we would never tell.

Slay the Dragon: By Ian

That was it. The doctor told us Keith was dead. I should have been sad. I should have shown some emotion. But I couldn't. He had to die. Now she was free.